"It's been a good week for me, Clara," Ethan said.

Clara blushed. "For me, too."

"If I had known how much easier my life would be with a nanny I would have hired one weeks ago."

A nanny. Any nanny. Not specially Clara Barkman. She couldn't suppress the small twinge his words caused, but she quickly told herself it didn't matter. She wasn't seeking praise. He was right. Another woman could have done the job as well as she. It was prideful to think otherwise. If she was hired as the new teacher, another woman would take her place with this family.

No one mentioned that Clara might become too attached to the family. She needed to keep her emotions in check. She was the nanny, nothing more.

"Is everything all right, Clara?" Ethan was watching her closely.

"Of course," she managed to say.

Ethan was slowly finding his way to becoming a parent, and she was glad for him. He would be a good father if he just gave himself a chance. He needed someone to believe in him.

Books by Patricia Davids

Love Inspired

His Bundle of Love
Love Thine Enemy
Prodigal Daughter
The Color of Courage
Military Daddy
A Matter of the Heart
A Military Match
A Family for Thanksgiving
**Katie's Redemption*
**The Doctor's Blessing*
**An Amish Christmas*
**The Farmer Next Door*
**The Christmas Quilt*
**A Home for Hannah*
**A Hope Springs Christmas*
**Plain Admirer*
**Amish Christmas Joy*
**The Shepherd's Bride*
**The Amish Nanny*

*Brides of Amish Country

Love Inspired Suspense

A Cloud of Suspicion
Speed Trap

PATRICIA DAVIDS

After thirty-five years as a nurse, Pat hung up her stethoscope to become a full-time writer. She enjoys spending her new free time visiting her grandchildren, doing some long-overdue yard work and traveling to research her story locations. She resides in Wichita, Kansas. Pat always enjoys hearing from her readers. You can visit her online at www.patriciadavids.com.

The Amish Nanny

Patricia Davids

Recycling programs for this product may not exist in your area.

ISBN-13: 978-0-373-81781-8

THE AMISH NANNY

This edition published by arrangement with Love Inspired Books.

www.Harlequin.com

Printed in U.S.A.

Who can find a virtuous woman?
For her price is far above rubies.
—*Proverbs* 31:10

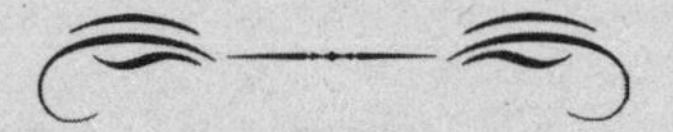

The book is lovingly dedicated to teachers everywhere.
The hardest job in the world brings forth
the greatest rewards.

Chapter One

Ethan Gingerich led his draft horses out of their stalls and started to slide open the large door of his barn, but he stopped when he saw two irate women standing just outside. At second glance, only the one gripping his nephew Micah's collar looked irate. It was Faith Lapp, his neighbor's wife. He didn't recognize the pretty young woman standing behind Faith. She looked scared. Her bright blue eyes were wide with apprehension.

Faith pointed to the child in her grasp. "Ethan Gingerich, do you know what your boy has done?"

He'd never seen the mild-mannered woman with such fire in her eyes. And what was that horrible smell? It seemed to be coming from his nephew. "I reckon I'd be the one holding him by the collar if I knew. What did you do this time, *sohn?*"

Micah glared at him. "I'm not your son."

"That's neither here nor there. You did something to upset Mrs. Lapp. What was it?"

Micah looked down at his bare toes. "Nothing."

Faith let go of his shirt and gestured toward the woman standing with her. "This is my friend Clara Barkman. Clara saw him jump out of a tree onto one of my alpacas."

Ethan flinched. He'd heard stories about the way Faith Lapp valued her strange animals. She treated them almost like family. How much would an alpaca cost if he had to replace one? He could barely afford to feed the family and his horses as it was. He hadn't been able to go logging in weeks. Not since his brother's children had come to live with him over a month ago. No cut timber to sell meant zero income.

Micah raked his bare toes through the dirt. "I just wanted to ride one. I didn't mean any harm."

Faith scowled at him. "They're very delicate animals. They can't carry a rider bigger than a two-year-old. Had you asked permission to ride one of them, I would have told you that. You could have seriously injured Myrtle."

"Or you might have been injured yourself," Clara added in a small voice.

He liked that she was thinking of the child. The recent deaths of his brother and sister-in-law had left him in charge of their three small children. He gazed at Micah's belligerent face. They were still finding their way with each other. Micah was having a much harder time than his younger brother and sister.

The boy was only eight, but he wasn't too young to learn responsibility and respect. "Micah will work off any damages that are owed, Mrs. Lapp. Go up to the house, boy. We'll talk about this later."

Micah's chin came up. "I'm not scared of you."

Ethan managed to keep a stern face, but it was difficult. Micah was so much like his father had been at that age. Always ready to scrap with his bigger, older brother. Ethan summoned a forbidding tone. "You should be. Don't make me tell you twice. Go!"

Micah's defiance crumbled. He bolted toward the house. The fire in Faith Lapp's eyes cooled as she watched the boy race up the front porch steps. Her expression turned to one of sympathy when she looked back at Ethan. "I know how troubled a boy can be when he has lost his parents as Micah has. It was the same with my nephew when Kyle first came to me. It takes time, and it takes attention to help them recover."

Why did women always think he needed a lecture on how to manage the children? He'd already had plenty of that from his aunts. Was he ever to have any peace? "I'll handle Micah in my own way. Is there anything else?"

He shoved the barn door wide open and led his

team of draft horses out. Faith moved aside, but Clara shrieked and threw up her hands as she scurried backward, almost falling in her haste. The horses snorted and tossed their heads, jerking him off the ground for an instant. Terror-stricken, Clara covered her face with her hands. What was wrong with her?

He calmed his animals. "Easy, boys, easy."

Faith wrapped her arm around Clara's shoulders and moved her to the side. "Clara is frightened by large horses. Would you take them away, please, Mr. Gingerich?"

"An Amish woman who is afraid of horses?" He would have laughed at the idea, but the proof of it was cowering before him.

"Only big ones," Clara admitted breathlessly. She had her eyes scrunched shut.

"These are big," he acknowledged as he led them past the women to the nearby pasture gate. He owned two teams of massive Belgians, among the largest of all draft horse breeds. They were his most prized possessions. He loved their strength and their power, their placid nature and their willingness to work as hard as he asked without flagging. How could anyone be afraid of such gentle giants?

When he turned them loose in the pasture, Fred and Dutch took off at a thundering gallop, bucking like colts and nipping playfully at each other. He never grew tired of watching the matching sorrels with their sleek red-brown coats and blond manes and tails. They were beautiful to behold.

But he had more than his horses to look after now. He had three *kinder* to care for. One of them was bent on getting himself into trouble at every turn. Ethan came back to stand by Faith. Now that the horses were gone, Clara had her eyes open. It was easy to see she was embarrassed by her reaction. Her cheeks were bright red. Her gaze was focused on her hands clasped tightly in front of her. "I'm sorry I made a fuss. I wasn't expecting to see them."

He took pity on her. "My sister-in-law would shriek at the sight of the tiniest spider in the house. Everyone is afraid of something."

Clara gave him a tremulous smile, a reward for his kindness. "My father's team of draft horses bolted and ran over me when I was six."

"Were you badly hurt?" he asked.

The bright color was fading from her cheeks. "*Nee,* their big feet missed me by the grace of God."

"It's not so surprising. My teams pay close attention to where they put their hooves. They don't like to be tripped up. But you didn't come to talk about horses. What kind of damages do I owe for the injury to your animal, Mrs. Lapp?"

"Myrtle seems to be all right. She had a bad

fright more than anything. She may be skittish for a few days, but I think she'll recover.

"You let me know if she starts ailing. I'll send Micah to work for you for the next three days, if that's agreeable."

"If you are sure you don't need him here."

"I can spare him for the mornings. Is that acceptable?"

Faith nodded. "*Ja,* it is. Perhaps if he learns more about alpacas, he'll be careful around them. I'm afraid Myrtle spit on him. It will take a few days of airing for the smell to get out of his clothes."

"Serves him right. I'll see that he's punished for what he did."

Clara's gaze snapped up and locked with his for an instant before she looked down again. "He's only a little boy."

"He's old enough to know better. I don't tolerate careless or wild behavior around my animals. He knows that. If there's nothing else, I've got two more horses that need to go out to pasture. They're big ones, too," he added.

Clara flinched at his remark. He regretted sounding short-tempered, but before he could form some kind of apology, the women turned and walked away.

His eyes stayed on the gently swaying figure of Clara as she and Faith went down the lane. Clara Barkman. He wasn't familiar with the name. Was she a local woman? He didn't attend the same church group as his neighbors, so he hadn't seen her before.

She stopped and glanced back for a moment. He raised a hand to wave. She suddenly rushed to catch up with Faith. He watched until they rounded the bend in the road, but she didn't look back again. She was a pretty woman. Was she married?

He shoved aside the thought. It didn't matter. He wasn't interested in her or any woman. Clara might be pretty, but a pretty face didn't mean much. He had loved one beautiful woman beyond all reason. She said that she loved him, too, but she had married another man. A man he had introduced her to… His best friend. Their betrayal of his trust cut deep. He didn't know if it would ever heal although he tried his best to forgive them.

Jenny's beautiful face hid a selfish nature. She decided not to settle for a poor fellow with only his horses and his heart to offer her. She wanted a secure life. She found it with a man who owned a big house and his own factory. An *Englisch* man. That she had to turn her back on her Amish faith hadn't deterred her any more than it had kept his mother from leaving.

Ethan rubbed his hand over his chest, but it didn't lessen the ache those memories caused.

He returned to the barn and brought Rosie and Golda out. After checking them over, he turned them loose in the pasture, too. Golda took off at a gallop to catch up with the boys, but pregnant Rosie buried her nose in the long grass and began tearing up mouthfuls near his feet. He patted her sleek shoulder. "Eat good, little *mudder.* I need a strong, healthy *hutsh* from you."

Rosie and her colt would be the foundation of his business as a draft horse breeder and trainer. Up until now, he'd made a living by logging, but with the addition of the children in his life, he needed a way to earn a living that didn't take him away from home for much of the fall and early winter. It was his new plan for the future, but he knew God had a way of changing a man's plans without warning.

He settled his hat lower on his brow as he glanced toward the house, where Micah was waiting for him. He'd never expected to raise his niece and nephews. He drew comfort from knowing he was doing what his brother would have wanted, but he hadn't realized how hard it would be. For everyone.

What could he say to make Micah understand he was traveling down the wrong path? Ethan looked up at the cloudless blue sky. "God, I don't know why You needed my brother and his wife with You, but we sure do miss them. If You want me to look after their *kinder,* You had better show me the way to make it work, Lord, because right now I'm lost."

He shook off the sadness that made his eyes sting. He wouldn't dwell on his loss. He couldn't afford to let grief muddle his thinking. Work would help clear his head.

He turned away from the house and entered the barn. Micah could stew a few minutes. Grabbing a pitchfork, he began tossing fresh straw into the stalls. He needed to find the right thing to say to Micah. More important, he needed to find a way to take care of all the children that didn't involve sending them to live with their only other family members.

Ethan refused to consider sending them to his mother. She had given up her Amish faith and any right to be considered part of the family when she left his father. Ethan did have two elderly aunts willing to take one child each, but they wanted to leave Micah with him. He couldn't do that to them.

Separating the *kinder* was something he knew his brother wouldn't want. Not after the way they had been torn apart as children.

Clara resisted the urge to glance over her shoulder again as she and Faith walked away from Ethan's home. What kind of punishment did he have planned for Micah? She flinched at the memory of her uncle taking a strap to her back.

Like Micah, she and her sisters had been taken in by their uncle after their parents died. Their uncle Morris was a weak, cruel man. He made their lives miserable for years. The final straw came when he tried to force her to marry a horrible man. By the grace of God and with the bravery of her sister Lizzie, they were able to escape. Now they lived with their grandfather in the Amish community of Hope Springs, Ohio. Clara tried hard to put her unhappy past behind her, but sometimes it came back to haunt her. Like now.

She knew not every man was cruel. Faith's husband was a wonderful, kind husband and father, but Ethan Gingerich looked and sounded so stern. She glanced at Faith. "Do you think Micah will be all right?"

"He wasn't hurt in the fall. Why wouldn't he be all right?"

Clara kept her pace slow to match Faith's limping stride. Faith wore a brace on one leg due to an old injury. "Did Micah's *onkel* seem angry to you? He seemed very angry to me."

"I could see he was disappointed in the boy's behavior. That's to be expected."

"What do you know about him?"

"Not much really. He keeps to himself. He moved here about two years ago. He makes a living logging with his horses. He lived alone until recently. One day last month, he stopped by to ask Adrian to look after his horses while he went to Indiana for a funeral. Apparently, his brother and his brother's wife were struck and killed by lightning while they were working in the field. It was a terrible tragedy.

Ethan brought their children back to live with him. I took some food to them when they first arrived. The poor children looked so lost. I should've gone back to visit."

"You've had your hands full with the new baby."

"That's true, but it's no excuse for being a poor neighbor. I hope their church has been helping."

They rounded a bend in the road, and Clara couldn't see the house behind them anymore. A large cornfield blocked her view. The sea of green leaves and golden tassels danced in the wind making rattling, hissing sounds as the stiff leaves slapped against each other.

Would Ethan slap Micah?

The boy was so small, and Ethan was a big man. He could easily hurt the child. She dreaded to think Micah was being punished because she was the one who saw him jump on Myrtle. She had been so startled that she had immediately called Faith to the window. If only she had remained silent. The boy would have gone home, and no one would have known about his actions. But that wouldn't have been right, either.

She prayed Ethan would deal with Micah kindly, but not knowing troubled her. The Amish were gentle people. She knew that, but evil could lurk among the good. Her uncle was proof of that. Her heart started pounding painfully as she remembered his cruelty.

She stopped in the roadway and clasped her arms across her middle as she closed her eyes. Images of her uncle raising his wooden rod to strike her flashed into her mind and she braced for the blow. Was Micah's uncle as cruel as hers had been? It wasn't likely, but what if he was?

"What is it, Clara?"

Clara opened her eyes and saw the concern on her friend's face. She drew a shaky breath. That part of her life was over. She and her three sisters were safe. Their uncle couldn't hurt them anymore. She had to remind herself of that fact every day. After years of fear and meekness, of striving desperately to please her uncle and failing, it was sometimes hard to believe God had finally answered her prayers. Was Micah praying for deliverance from his uncle's wrath, too? She had to know.

She couldn't leave without knowing.

"Faith, would you mind if we called it quits early today?"

"Of course not. Are you okay?"

"I'm fine. My sisters are putting up corn this afternoon. I know they could use my help. I'll walk home from here."

"It will take more than one day to put up corn for your family. Take tomorrow off, too. Why don't we get together again on Saturday?"

Clara took two steps backward. She wanted to race back to the Gingerich farm, but she didn't want to arouse Faith's suspicions. "Are you sure you want me to come back? We've only a few more hours of spinning to do, and then we'll be done with this year's fleece."

"Please do come. I've enjoyed working with you so much. I want one last day together even if it's only for a few hours."

"All right. I'll see you Saturday morning." Clara turned and hurried back the way they had come, but instead of going home, she stopped at the bend in the road that led to Ethan's farm.

She rubbed her damp palms on the sides of her dress. What reason would she give for returning? She could hardly tell a man she'd just met that she feared he beat his children. Even if she saw him punishing Micah, what right did she have to interfere? None.

Yet how could she stand by and do nothing? It was partly her fault the boy was in trouble. If only she knew what was happening to the child.

Ethan might be a kind and fair guardian. Her Amish faith dictated that she see only the good in every man until shown otherwise. She certainly had no business suspecting Ethan Gingerich of evil, but she had to know that Micah was all right. Her life and her sister's lives might have been so much better if someone had cared enough to check on them.

None of them had admitted their abuse to anyone. They had been too ashamed to speak of it. Only her sister Lizzie had been strong enough to break thc pattern by running away. She found a wonderful home for them with their grandfather. She freed them all and saved Clara from being forced to marry an odious man.

She shuddered at the thought of what her life might have been like without her sister's bravery. God put more courage in Lizzie's little finger than Clara had in her whole body.

She glanced at the cornfield separating her from Ethan's home. She might not be brave, but a child's welfare could be at stake. She couldn't turn away from that.

Gathering what small courage she possessed, Clara moved off the road and into the cornfield beside the lane. The tall green stalks would hide her from view. If her suspicions were groundless, Ethan need never know she had come back to check on him.

The corn patch ended a few dozen yards from the back of the house. With her heart pounding in her throat, she ran across the open strip of grass and flattened herself against the back wall of the house. Had she been seen? She waited for sounds of discovery.

It was the height of summer, so the windows were all open to catch the slightest breeze. She heard the sound of voices coming from the window near the north corner of the building. Ducking low, she passed beneath one window and stopped under the next. Two more steps would put her beside the front porch. She thought the kitchen must be on the other side of the wall where she crouched.

"I'm asking for an explanation, Micah. Now's your chance to set the record straight."

Only silence followed Ethan's words. She strained to hear Micah's reply.

"What were you thinking?"

Clara nearly jumped out of her skin. Ethan had moved to stand beside the window where she was hunkering. He was directly above her. She squeezed her eyes shut and tried not to breathe.

Please, Lord, don't let him see me.

Finally, she heard heavy footsteps moving away, followed by the scrape of a chair across the floor. She took a badly needed breath. Ethan said, "Micah, what am I to do with you?"

"Are you going to send me away?"

It was the first she had heard from the boy. He didn't sound as if he was in pain, but she heard the worry under his words.

"Nee."

"Because no one wants me?"

"Why do you say that?"

"I overheard Great *Aenti* May say that she would take Lily if Great *Aenti* Carol would take Amos. Neither of them wanted to take me."

Clara pressed a hand to her lips. The poor child. To know he wasn't wanted had to hurt deeply.

Ethan cleared his throat. "I'm not sending any of you away. Your papa wanted all of you to stay together. Your actions today show your disrespect for his memory more clearly than words. How would he feel if Mrs. Lapp came to him to complain you injured one of her animals? Your papa loved animals."

Why didn't Ethan tell the boy he wanted him? It was what the child needed to hear. Clara knew how it felt to be unwanted and unloved. Her heart broke for Micah.

"I reckon I'd get a spanking for what I did."

"I reckon you would if he was here. Go to your room and think on how disappointed he would be with you. Send your brother and your sister down. You will sit and reflect alone and in silence."

"They aren't upstairs."

"Are you sure?"

"I checked before you came in."

"Where are they?" Ethan demanded.

"I don't know."

A chair scraped again. "Lily! Amos! Where are you?" There was an edge of panic in Ethan's voice. She heard his boots pounding up the stairs inside.

He wasn't going to beat Micah. She'd put herself in this foolish position for nothing. Now was her chance to leave, but what if he looked out one of the upstairs windows and saw her running across the lawn? Should she risk it? Could she make the cornfield before she was spotted?

Suddenly, she heard a childish giggle that was quickly smothered. It came from under the porch. Clara noticed a small opening in the latticework where the porch met the house. Looking through the gap, she saw a little girl of about four sitting cross-legged in the dirt with her hands clasped over her mouth. A boy a little older was seated behind her.

Taking her hands away from her mouth, the little girl pouted. "Oh, you found us."

"What are you doing under there?" Clara whispered. She could hear Ethan calling for them from the upstairs.

"We're playing hide-and-seek. We're hiding from *Onkel* Ethan."

That was exactly what Clara wanted to do. She heard his footsteps pound down the stairs. Now was her chance to run. "Micah, check out back," he yelled.

No! If Micah was out back, she couldn't pass him without being seen, and he was certain to recognize her.

In a few seconds, Ethan would be on the front porch. He was sure to check along this side of the house. He would find her snooping like a thief outside his home. How would she explain herself?

She couldn't. There was only one choice.

She smiled at the two children and pleaded, "May I join your game?"

They nodded. She quickly wiggled into the opening and held her breath as the front door banged open above her.

Chapter Two

Ethan came out onto his front porch and stood with his hands on his hips as he scanned the yard for the missing children. How could they disappear so quickly? He couldn't keep an eye on them every minute. How did mothers manage when they had half a dozen or more to keep track of every day?

He'd seen both Amos and Lily less than an hour ago. They had been playing on the swing set in the backyard until he sent them inside to clean their rooms. In the meanwhile, he'd gone out to care for his horses. Then he had been sidetracked by Faith Lapp and her pretty, shy friend Clara.

He called for Amos and Lily again but got no answer. Where should he search first? The barn? The henhouse? The creek? Where would a five-year-old and a four-year-old decide to go without telling him?

"Do you see them?" Micah asked as he came jogging around from the back of the house.

"*Nee.* Do you have any idea where they might be? Did they go with you to the Lapp farm?" He would send Micah back to the neighbors and enlist their aid if he couldn't find the children soon.

Please, Lord, don't let anything have happened to them.

"I went by myself. I didn't want them tagging along," Micah said.

"Are you sure they didn't follow you?"

The boy shrugged. "I guess they could have, but I didn't see them."

"You go check the henhouse and the other outbuildings. I'll check the barn. Maybe they're playing up in the hayloft and can't hear me calling."

"I thought you wanted me to go to my room."

Ethan scowled at his nephew in renewed annoyance. "After we find your brother and sister."

"They're probably just hiding from you."

That took Ethan aback. "Why would they hide from me?"

"Because they like to play hide-and-seek."

"Since when?"

"Since always. You just never pay attention to them." Micah jumped off the porch and strode toward the henhouse.

Ethan raked a hand through his hair. The boy was right. He paid attention to his horses and to his work. He loved his brother's children, but he didn't know them. He headed toward the barn and prayed the two little ones hadn't gone to the Lapp farm. He really did not want to face Faith and Clara again with more of his wayward children in tow.

Through the white painted latticework that bordered the porch, Clara watched Ethan enter the large red barn that stood fifty yards east of the house. The moment he was out of sight, she wiggled backward from beneath the porch. She motioned to the two children to come out, as well. "The game is over now. Your *onkel* is worried because he can't find you. I want you both to wait for him on the porch steps."

The little boy frowned and shook his head. "He didn't say *alle alle achts und frei.*"

How could he call for everyone to come in because they were free? The poor man wasn't aware that the game was on. How long would the pair have remained hidden? She didn't want Ethan to find out. "I will say it. *Alle alle achts und frei.*"

"We won." Lily beamed as she crawled out. She was covered with dirt and cobwebs. Her brother followed her in a similar state. Clara suspected that she looked the same.

"*Ja,* you won. You found the perfect hiding place." Were these little ones scared of Ethan? Was that why they were hiding?

Clara brushed them off as best she could and glanced toward the barn. There was no sign of Ethan, but he could reappear at any moment. "Why were you hiding from your *onkel?*"

"'Cause we like to play hide-and-seek."

"Why didn't you tell him you were playing with him?"

"I told him I wanted to play hide-and-seek," Amos said, but his gaze was on his bare toes.

"And what did he say?" she prompted.

"He said to clean our rooms," he admitted.

"We did and then we hid," Lily added with a grin.

Clara glanced toward the barn again. She had to get going. "Next time, you must make sure he knows he is playing the game before you hide."

"We will," Lily said with a nod.

Clara smiled at her. "Promise you'll stay on the porch until your *onkel* returns?"

"We promise," Amos said.

Lily nodded solemnly. "Will you come and play with us again?"

"Maybe, but today is our little secret, right? We won't tell anyone about our hiding place."

"We won't tell," Amos assured her.

"Danki." Clara couldn't waste any more time. After checking and not seeing Ethan or Micah, she scurried around the corner of the house and ran across the lawn into the cornfield. She pushed

through the thick green leaves and between the stalks as she rushed on. Even when she reached the road, she didn't slow down until she was a good half mile away from the farm.

A stitch in her side finally brought her to a halt. She looked back as she struggled to catch her breath. There was no sign of Ethan Gingerich. She was safe.

Grateful to escape from an extremely embarrassing situation of her own making without being discovered, she breathed a silent prayer of thanks. Just the thought of Ethan finding her lurking under his porch made her cringe. She wouldn't have had to worry about keeping her dignity intact because she would have died of embarrassment on the spot.

It would have served her right to be found hiding like a mongrel dog. She had doubted the goodness of Ethan Gingerich. To do so was wrong and showed the weakness of her faith. It was something she strived to overcome with prayer, but she had a long way to go.

Not all men were like her uncle and the ruthless man he tried to make her marry. Ethan wasn't cruel. He might not know how to handle the children, but he wasn't unkind to them.

She glanced over her shoulder once more and began walking quickly toward her grandfather's sheep farm. She hadn't told the children her name. She had to pray they wouldn't figure out who she was and tell Ethan about her actions. Hopefully, she wouldn't have to face him again for a long, long time.

When Ethan came out of the barn after checking every hiding place he could think of he saw Lily and Amos sitting on the front steps of the house. They were safe. He strode toward them, his relief quickly turning to frustration and annoyance. He had wasted a large part of his morning dealing with first one child and then the others.

He stopped in front of the steps and crossed his arms. "Where have you been? Didn't you hear me calling you?"

Lily and Amos exchanged guilty glances. Amos said, "We heard you."

"Why didn't you answer me?"

"That's not the way to play the game," Lily explained.

Ethan gave her a stern look. "Exactly what game were you playing? Give *Onkel* Ethan gray hair?"

Lily shook her head. "I don't know that game."

Ethan drew a hand down his face to wipe away his grin. He struggled to keep a firm tone. "Were you playing hide-and-seek?"

She smiled brightly. "*Ja,* and we won."

Amos grinned, too. "You never found us."

"The next time you decide to play hide-and-seek you must make sure that I know you're playing."

The smile vanished from Lily's face and she sighed heavily. "That's what our friend said."

Amos elbowed her in the side. "That's a secret."

Her eyes widened and she clapped a hand to her mouth. "I forgot," she mumbled.

Ethan glanced around for another child but didn't see one. "Was there someone else playing with you? Who was it?"

Amos pressed his lips into a thin line and folded his arms tightly. Lily glanced at him and did the same.

Baffled by their refusal to answer him, he stared at their set faces. Should he demand they tell him who else was playing with them? Did it matter? It did if a child was hiding somewhere and his or her parents didn't know where. He would have to try a different tactic.

He glanced at the position of the sun in the sky. "It's almost lunchtime. Are you two hungry?"

"I sure am." Amos jumped to his feet.

"Me, too. Can we have macaroni and cheese?" Lily asked.

"I reckon that'll be as good a meal as any." It was something he could fix without much fuss. Thankfully, the children hadn't tired of it.

"Yum!" Lily's big grin sent warmth shooting through his chest. She was an adorable child. She looked so much like her mother. It was up to him to see that she grew into a modest and devout woman, too. The thought filled him with dread. He had no idea how to accomplish that feat.

"Will your friend want some, too?" he asked, casually glancing around again for another child.

"She's gone home," Lily said, heading toward the door.

Micah ambled across the yard and stopped beside Ethan. He shoved his hands deep in his pockets. "I see you found them. Are you going to give them a spanking?"

Lily spun around looking horrified. She held her hands over her backside. "I don't want a spanking."

Ethan shook his head. "No one is getting spanked. But Micah is going to his room to think about what he did wrong today. After lunch, you little ones can go play on the swings, but I don't want you to leave the backyard without telling me. Is that understood?"

They both nodded solemnly, but he had to wonder as he held open the door for them just how long they would remember his instructions.

Clara sat in Faith's workroom on Saturday morning and spun the final carding of fleece into fine strands of yarn. She glanced out the window, but the branches of the tree overhanging the alpacas' pen were empty. The animals grazed peacefully beneath it.

She hadn't mentioned her meeting with Ethan

or her return visit to his farm to her family. She preferred to forget about her foolish behavior and put it behind her, but she constantly found herself wondering how Ethan was doing. Not that it was any of her business. Still, even knowing that didn't keep thoughts of him at bay. He needed help with those children. She hoped he wasn't too proud to ask for it.

Faith came in from the kitchen. "Are you finished already?"

"That is the last of it." Clara stopped the wheel and handed a spindle full of white alpaca yarn to Faith.

Faith took it and added it to an overflowing basket. "I'm glad to be done, but I am truly going to miss your company, Clara. I never would have finished in time without you. These orders can go out tomorrow."

Faith's husband, Adrian, came in holding their three-month-old daughter, Ruby. "Micah Gingerich is here. He says that you have chores you want him to do?"

"Indeed I have." Faith sprang to her feet and marched out of the room.

Adrian laughed. "Never mess with that woman's child or her alpacas."

Clara held out her arms. "May I hold Ruby for a while? I will miss the time I've spent with you and with Faith, but it is this little one that I shall miss the most of all."

He handed the sleeping baby to her. "I had better go see what jobs Faith is assigning to Micah. It's always best when the grown-ups present a unified front."

Clara held the baby close as Adrian left the room. She would miss being here more than she cared to admit. She loved babies. The Lord had found a beautiful way to begin people. Children were a constant reminder of God's love and grace in the world.

Clara's one great sadness was that she would never hold a babe of her own. The idea of marriage was utterly repugnant after her treatment at the hands of her would-be fiancé. No, she would remain single. She took a seat in the rocker and cuddled the baby until Faith returned.

Smiling, Faith crossed the room. "I'll take her now."

"Are you sure I can't take her home with me?"

Faith propped her hands on her hips. "I could let you, but you'll bring her back about three o'clock in the morning."

"My sisters and I have raised a dozen bottle lambs on our grandfather's farm this spring. I think we could manage this little lamb, too."

Faith lifted the babe from her arms. "I'm sure you could. You will have babes of your own someday. Is there any young man in our community who has caught your fancy?" Faith asked with a quick peek in Clara's direction and a knowing smile.

"*Nee,* marriage isn't for me." Clara looked down and didn't elaborate. Oddly, Ethan's face popped into her head. He needed a wife to look after his children.

Why should she think of him now?

Faith took a seat in the chair beside her. "I know some of your story, Clara. I know you escaped marriage to a brutal man by running away on your wedding day."

Clara looked up, startled. "How did you find out?"

"Your sister Lizzie told me about it."

"It was by the grace of God and by my sister Lizzie's determination to save me that I was spared a life of hopelessness and pain." Clara laid a hand to her cheek as she remembered the painful slap of Rufus's heavy hand striking her.

Faith nodded. "Lizzie was very brave to travel all the way from Indiana to Hope Springs on her own. She was determined to find a place for you and your sisters to live. We are all thankful that she convinced your grandfather to take you in."

"No one is more thankful than I am. Lizzie is the brave one. I could never have done what she did. If Rufus Kuhns had been determined to marry her instead of me, I wouldn't have been able to save her."

"You don't know that," Faith said gently.

"*Ja,* I do."

"Is it true that Lizzie is going to marry your grandfather's hired man in the fall?"

Relieved to speak of something else, Clara smiled. *"Ja."*

"Carl King seems like a good man."

Clara bit the corner of her lip. "I think he is."

"You think, but you aren't sure?"

Was she that transparent? Over the past few months, as the women had worked side by side in the bright and cheerful room, Clara had shared some of her life and had learned some of Faith's story, as well. Faith's first husband had been an abusive man. She had been a widow when she moved to Hope Springs.

Clara looked up and gazed intently into Faith's eyes. "How did you know that Adrian wouldn't turn out to be cruel, too? Weren't you afraid?"

Faith smiled gently. "Of course I was. I felt as you do. I thought I would never be able to trust another man, but Adrian changed all that the first time he touched my face. There was so much gentleness in that touch. I knew he would never hurt me. I understand your fear, but there are good men, kind men, men who spend a lifetime loving their wives and being helpmates. You will find one."

The very idea of submitting to a husband turned her insides cold. "My head tells me what you say is right, but I don't feel that way. And this conversation has no point because there is no one interested in courting me. I should be getting home. I told Lizzie that I would help her finish canning corn this afternoon."

"I understand. I'll pray for you, Clara. I will pray that God has someone special in mind for you."

Clara gathered her things together. "Pray that I get hired as the new schoolteacher. That's what I truly want to do. I want to teach and take care of dozens of children. I can't imagine a more perfect job."

"Okay, I'll do that, too. I'll see you again at the Sunday's service."

The two women kissed each other's cheeks, and Clara left the room. Outside, she saw Micah carrying a large armload of alfalfa hay toward the alpacas' enclosure. She crossed the yard toward him. "Good day, Micah. I'm glad to see you have come to do chores as you promised."

"My *onkel* promised I would come. I didn't."

His sullen expression worried her. "Your *onkel* was right in this. Your punishment could have been much worse."

"Worse than the whipping I took? I doubt it. A lot you care. You're the one who got me in trouble."

"You got into trouble all by yourself, Micah. You have no reason to blame me. I seriously doubt that your *onkel* Ethan gave you a whipping."

"He did. The minute you left he…he paddled me so hard I couldn't sit down for hours."

Clara folded her arms over her chest. "You are a very poor liar, Micah Gingerich."

"I am not!"

She arched her eyebrow. "You're not a poor liar? Then I reckon that makes you a good liar."

He scowled at her. "I've got to go feed those stupid animals." He trudged away without looking at her again.

She shook her head and muttered under her breath, "Poor Ethan. You really have your hands full with this one."

How would he manage? It was painfully clear the boy was determined to tread the wrong path. Such defiance in one so young did not bode well for the family.

As she watched Micah enter the corral, she saw him spread out the hay, then slowly reach his hand toward one of the babies in the group who had come close to investigate. The hopeful expression on Micah's face told her he liked the alpacas even if he wouldn't admit it.

The baby stretched his nose toward Micah. The tentative exchange was cut short when Myrtle alerted the rest of the herd with a shrill whistling sound. The baby and all the others scampered away from Micah to the opposite side of the corral. He kicked the hay at his feet and stomped off.

Clara left the Lapp farm and walked toward her grandfather's home. As she followed the winding country road, she couldn't stop thinking about Micah's attitude and Ethan's inability to connect with the boy. Was there some way she could help?

She didn't see how. Her job with Faith was finished for this summer. She wouldn't be back to see how Micah faired with his week of chores unless she simply came for a visit.

Since the Gingeriches were members of a different church congregation, Micah wouldn't attend the school where she hoped to teach. If she got the job, and if he were one of her students, she would have some contact and influence over him, but she couldn't see a way to spend time with the troubled boy as things stood now.

She was crossing the small bridge that spanned Cherry Creek just beyond Ethan's lane when she heard a familiar giggle. She stopped and peered over the railing. Lily and Amos were knee-deep in the muddy water below her. She quickly looked around for Ethan, but he was nowhere in sight.

She leaned her arms on the railing. "What are you doing?"

Lily looked up at her and grinned. She held a huge frog in her hands. The front of her dress was covered in mud and slime "See what I caught?"

"I see. That's a beautiful frog."

Amos was creeping toward the bank with his hands outstretched. "I'm going to get me one, too."

He launched himself toward the shore. The bullfrog that was his target leaped over his head and disappeared into the muddy depths of the creek.

Clara tried not to laugh. "Where is your *onkel?*"

"He's got a sick cow," Lily said. "He told us to go play."

"Do you think that he meant to go play in the creek? You are both very muddy."

Amos looked from the front of his clothes to his sister's sopping dress. "He didn't say not to play in the creek."

"I'm certain this is not what he had in mind. Come out of there."

"Can I keep my frog?" Lily asked hopefully.

"I think he will be happier if you leave him in his own home."

Amos waded to her side. "Let him go. We can catch him another time."

"Okay." She didn't look happy about it, but she put him back in the water and giggled as he quickly swam away.

The children climbed up to the road beside Clara. Lily reached for her hand. Clara flinched slightly but grasped the child's muddy fingers. Lily grinned at her. "What's your name?"

"I'm Clara Barkman."

"Have you come to play with us again?" She

gave a beaming smile that melted Clara's heart. What an adorable child she was.

"I'm just going to walk you home."

"We didn't tell about our hiding place," Amos assured her.

"That's good. Of course, if your *onkel* asks about it, you must tell him the truth." She didn't want the children to lie to cover up her foolishness. If Ethan found out, she would face the consequences.

Right now, she had two very muddy, wet children to deliver to his door. She wasn't looking forward to their meeting.

Chapter Three

"Come on, Olga. You can do it. Just push a couple more times."

Ethan had spent the better part of three hours helping his cow deliver her first calf. The calf had been turned wrong. It had been a monumental struggle to get it into the correct position. For a few tense hours, he thought he might lose them both. As it was, Olga was tiring after laboring all night. He pulled on the calf's front legs to help ease it out into the world. He wasn't sure it would survive, but he wanted to save both of them.

"Mr. Gingerich, may I have a word with you?"

He jerked his head around to see Clara Barkman standing outside the stall. Now what? Was Micah in trouble again? "I'm a little busy at the moment." He pulled harder on the front legs of the calf when he felt the cow straining.

"Your two littlest children were playing down at the creek."

"So?"

"They were in the creek."

He scowled at her. "Are they okay?"

"They are fine. Muddy from head to toe, but fine."

The calf came free, and he lowered it to the straw. "Come on, little one. Breathe."

It was a small heifer. She struggled weakly. He quickly cleared the nostrils with his gloves. Her tongue was purple. It didn't look good for her.

"I'll take care of the children," Clara said.

"Fine. Hand me that blanket." He pointed to the corner of the stall. She slipped in and handed him the coarse bundle of fabric. *"Danki."*

He wrapped the calf in it and began to dry her, rubbing vigorously to stimulate her breathing. She began to respond with deeper breaths and finally a weak bawl. The next time he looked up, Clara was gone.

He worked to get the calf breathing well then standing, and finally he guided her to her mother's udder for her first meal. When she latched on and began to nurse, he let out a sigh of relief. It looked as if she was going to be okay.

He watched them for a while to make sure mother and daughter were bonding and doing well, then he left the stall and walked up to the house. He didn't see Clara or the kids, but the sound of shrieks led him to the backyard.

Both his nephew and niece were sitting in a large blue plastic tub of soapy water and splashing each other. Clara was wringing out one of Lily's dresses at a second tub. She shook it open and carried it to the clothesline, where a row of dresses, shirts and pants already waved in the hot summer breeze.

Lily saw him first. "I caught a frog, *Onkel* Ethan. It was a big one. Amos didn't catch any. Clara made me let it go."

There was still a trace of mud on her head. He squatted beside the tub and picked up the sponge that floated between them. He gently rinsed her hair. Clara stood beside the clothesline with her gaze fastened to her feet and her hands clasped in front of her. He said, "That sounds like an exciting adventure. Are you supposed to go to the creek alone?"

"Amos was with me."

"I see. Amos, was it wise to take your sister to the creek without telling me?"

"I guess not," Amos admitted slowly.

"The creek is very deep in places. Can Lily swim?"

Amos looked at his sister. "Can you?"

She shook her head. "No, but the frogs swim really fast. I'm going to swim like a frog someday. You can teach me, *Onkel* Ethan."

Ethan smiled at her enthusiasm. Lily did everything with gusto. "I would if I could, but I don't know how to swim. I'll find someone to teach you pretty quick, but until I do, no more wading in the creek. It's dangerous."

Lily frowned at him. "Not even if Clara is with us?"

He looked at the shy beauty standing beside the fresh laundry. "I think God was looking out for you today by sending Clara along when He did. I'm grateful to Him and to her."

"She's lots of fun. She plays with us," Lily said with a big grin for her new friend.

He stood and faced Clara. "She's a very nice lady. I see she has washed all your clothes, too. We'd better thank her properly."

Amos tipped his head to the side. "How do we do that?"

"Why don't we ask her if we can give her a ride home so she doesn't have to walk all the way in this heat?"

Amos rose to his feet. A stream of soap suds slid down his belly. "Miss Barkman, may we offer you a ride home?"

Ethan watched Clara struggle not to laugh. His nephew's gallant offer was a bit comical considering his lack of attire. Ethan picked up a nearby towel, wrapped it around the boy and lifted him from the tub.

Lily stood, and Clara wrapped her in a towel before lifting her out of the water, too. As they faced each other with the children in their arms, Ethan wished he could see Clara's eyes, but she wouldn't look at him. He waited for her to speak.

Finally, she nodded. "A ride would be nice. I live with my grandfather, Joseph Shetler. Do you know him?"

"The one they call Woolly Joe, the sheep farmer? I've been by the place. It's a long walk from here. I thought you lived with the Lapp family."

"I worked for Faith Lapp. I'm a spinner, but my job there is finished for the year. I hope you don't mind that I bathed the children out here. I didn't want them trudging through the house in the state they were in."

"It looks like a good idea to me. Come on, kids. Let's get dressed and take Clara home."

"The children have only nightclothes to wear. I've washed all the rest. Nothing else was clean."

"I've been meaning to do their laundry," he admitted. Along with a dozen other chores he couldn't find time to get done.

She glanced at him, and he caught a glimpse of her stunning blue eyes before she dropped her gaze again. Her cheeks grew pale. "I didn't mean that as a criticism."

"I didn't take it as such. The children and I appreciate your neighborly gesture. *Danki.*"

"You are *wilkumm,*" she replied in a small voice.

"Micah should be home soon. We'll have lunch

when he gets here. The clothes should be dry by then, don't you think?"

She nodded without speaking. He hefted Amos to get a better hold on the boy and carried him toward the house. "Olga has had a new heifer. You children will have to help me name her."

"Let's call her Clara," Lily said. He heard Clara's bitten-off laughter quickly turn into a cough. It proved she had a sense of humor.

She said, "That's very sweet, Lily, but it might get confusing. What if you said you wanted to go picking strawberries with Clara and your *onkel* gave the calf a basket?"

Lily said, "That's silly."

"Let's choose a different name." Ethan held open the back door so that Clara could go inside. She hesitated, but then rushed past him. She was as skittish as a wild colt. Why was she afraid of him?

What on earth had possessed her to accept a ride home with Ethan? Clara had agreed because she didn't want to hurt Amos's feelings, but she hadn't thought about spending the next hour with Ethan watching her every move. He made her feel like jumping out of her skin.

"How about Heidi for a name?" Amos suggested.

Ethan set the boy on the floor and appeared to give the idea careful consideration. "Heidi the

Heifer. It has a certain ring to it. What do you think, Lily?"

Lily, still in Clara's arms, worked her hands out of the towel and cupped Clara's face. "I like it. Do you like it, Clara?"

Clara's heart turned over with a surge of emotion at the child's touch. What she wouldn't give to have a little girl of her own like Lily. "It's an excellent name. Let's go and put your nightgown on until your clothes get dry."

She carried the child up the stairs, happy to escape Ethan's watchful eyes.

Once in the girl's room, Clara finished drying the child and helped her dress in a white cotton nightgown with a tiny pink ribbon threaded through the lace at the neckline. "Sit down and let me comb and braid your hair."

Lily climbed on the bed and sat cross-legged with her toes peeking from beneath the hem of her gown. She tipped her head to the side. "Clara, will you be my friend?"

"I would be delighted to be your friend, Lily." Clara began to pull a comb gently through the girl's tangled hair.

"What do friends do?"

"Friends do all kinds of things together." She finished combing and began to braid the wet strands.

"Like what?"

"Friends visit each other. Sometimes they help

each other with problems. They play games. When you are older, you can go to quilting bees and singings and simply enjoy each other's company."

"Do you enjoy my company?"

Clara smiled. "Very much."

"I think I like having you for a friend."

Clara secured the end of Lily's braid with an elastic band. "I like having you for a friend, too."

"Do you want to play hide-and-seek?"

Clara flicked the end of Lily's nose with her finger. "*Nee,* for I have just got you clean. No hide-and-seek today."

"Tomorrow?"

Sitting on the bed beside the child, Clara said, "I won't be back tomorrow."

Lily's smile vanished. "Why not?"

"Because my job with the Lapp family is finished. I'm not sure when we will see each other again."

"But you are my friend, and I want you to play with me." Lily's lower lip began to quiver.

Clara wrapped her arms around the child. "We will plan a visit. How about that? Someday soon. I'll ask your *onkel* to bring you to my grandfather's farm so you can see all our sheep and meet our dog, Duncan."

"When?"

"I'll work that out with your *onkel,* but it won't be long."

"Promise?"

Ethan didn't seem to mind her giving the children a bath, but how would he feel about bringing Lily for a visit? Looking at the child's hopeful face, Clara decided to ask and hoped her courage wouldn't desert her when she was face-to-face with him. "I promise. Now smile for me. It makes my heart happy when I see a grin on your face."

Lily complied. Amos came upstairs still wrapped in his towel. She left him to get dressed in his room. When he came out in his pajamas, he had a wooden puzzle in his hands. "*Onkel* said we were to play up here until he calls us to eat."

"Okay." Lily slipped to the floor and the two of them began to assemble the puzzle on the blue-and-white braided rag rug beside her bed.

Clara went down to see what she could do to help Ethan. The kitchen smelled of cooking ham. Ethan stood at the stove with his back to her, frying the meat in a skillet. There was a freshly sliced loaf of bread on the table along with a bowl of tomatoes.

Clara saw that Micah was home. The boy was setting the table. He paused when he caught sight of Clara. "What's she doing here?"

"She has been taking care of your brother and sister."

"Spying on us, you mean. She's always spying."

Clara's stomach lurched. She pressed a hand to

her midsection. Her foolish behavior was about to be exposed.

Ethan turned from the stove to scowl at the boy. “Apologize to Clara right now, Micah.”

“But it’s true. She was watching me at the Lapp farm, waiting to get me in trouble. She was watching me again today. Now she’s here in our house.”

Clara’s knees went weak with relief. He didn’t seem to know about her return visit the first time she came here.

Ethan glanced at her and back to Micah. “Only someone doing wrong fears discovery. If you are afraid Clara will see you doing something wrong, then you must have something to hide.”

“Everyone thinks I’m bad.” Micah slammed down the plate and raced out of the house.

Ethan sighed heavily. “I apologize for my nephew’s behavior.”

Clara was more ashamed then ever by her suspicions about Ethan. “I wasn’t spying on Micah.”

“I know that.”

“I was spying on you.” She bowed her head, unable to face him.

“On me?”

She nodded. “I came back after Faith and I left the other day and I listened beneath the window to your conversation with Micah.”

“Why would you do that?”

Clara closed her eyes in shame. "I was afraid you would beat him."

He didn't reply. She chanced a look at him and saw disbelief written on his face. Quickly, she said, "When my parents died, my sisters and I went to live with our *onkel.* He wasn't kind."

"He was cruel to you?"

She nodded, unable to speak past the lump in her throat.

After a long pause, he said, "I see. Have your fears for my children been eased, or have I given you more to worry about?"

He was offended. She didn't blame him. She swallowed hard. "I was wrong, and I beg your forgiveness. I don't need that ride home. Tell the children I said goodbye."

She rushed out of the house before he could say anything else, before he could see the tears of shame that sprang to her eyes and trickled down her cheeks.

It was a long hot walk home, but Clara barely noticed the distance or the growing heat of the early July day. She was too humiliated to care about the sun beating down on her shoulders or the dust she kicked up on the road. It was unlikely that Ethan would bring Lily to visit her now. Although she had only met the children briefly, she was quite taken with Amos and Lily. She would have enjoyed seeing them again.

Clara looked up at the cloudless sky. It seemed that her poor behavior had cost her more than dented dignity. It was a hard lesson that she wouldn't soon forget.

When she finally reached her grandfather's home, she found her sisters hard at work. Lizzie stood at the stove sweating over a huge pan of simmering ears of corn. At the back of the stove, a pressure cooker began to whistle. Lizzie used a pair of thick oven mitts to move it off the heat. At the kitchen table, her youngest sister, Betsy, was cutting the kernels off the cobs into a bowl while Greta packed them into glass jars.

"Oh, good, you're home." Lizzie smiled brightly.

Surrounded by her family, Clara let go of her self-pity. She had made a mistake. It couldn't be undone. It couldn't be changed. Life went on. She would remember Ethan and his family in her prayers, but that was all she could do. Perhaps in time, he would forgive her, but she couldn't dwell on her blunders.

She looked around the room at the people who loved her and accepted her as she was.

"What can I do to help?" she asked, not wanting to think about Ethan anymore.

Lizzie checked the simmering corn ears with a long fork, then put the lid back on the kettle. "You can gather and shuck more ears for us. We've put up thirty pints, but we should hurry and put up thirty more before the corn hardens in this heat."

"Okay. Where is Naomi?" Clara asked.

Naomi was their grandfather's new wife. After years of loving each other from afar, the Lord had finally given them the courage to begin a new chapter of their lives together. All the girls adored her. It was easy to see how happy she made their grandfather.

"Naomi and *Daadi* have gone into town to visit Naomi's daughter. We got word this morning after you had gone that Emma had her baby."

"How wonderful. Is it a boy or a girl?" Clara asked even as she shook off a stab of jealousy. She wanted children, too, but that required a husband. After her narrow escape, she was content to remain single. Teaching would be her calling.

"Emma had a baby girl. She and Adam haven't decided on a name yet," Greta said.

Betsy tossed her empty cob into a bucket at her feet and picked up another ear of corn. "Naomi will be spending a week or two with them so she can help with the baby and with running the inn."

"How was your day, Clara?" Greta asked.

"It was fine. I'll go bring in some more corn." She didn't want to talk about Ethan and his family. Her embarrassment was too fresh in her mind.

Outside, she faced the corn patch Greta had

tended so carefully through the spring and early summer. A red wagon with an empty crate in it sat beside the garden gate. She took the handle and pulled it to the end of the row. Leaving the wagon, she walked in among the green stalks. The smell of the corn and the rustling of the broad leaves in the breeze were a painful reminder of her visit to spy on Ethan.

She grasped the first ear. The corn silk reminded her of Lily's baby-fine blond hair. Clara peeled back a strip of corn husk to reveal the kernels beneath. Using her thumbnail, she pressed into one. A small splatter of juice told her the ear was perfect for picking. She pulled both ears off the stalk and moved to the next plant.

Who would be canning corn for Ethan and his family? Perhaps some of the women in his church planned to do it for him. Or maybe he had family members who would come and take care of such things. She couldn't envision Ethan happily canning vegetables in his kitchen, but she knew there were men who enjoyed such tasks.

He would need a wife now that he had his brother's children to care for. Even her short time with his family was enough to see he needed a woman's touch in the home.

And why was she thinking about him again?

She sighed and kept working. It wasn't as easy to forget about him as she had hoped.

* * *

"I want Clara to do this." Lily sniffled and pulled the hairbrush from Ethan's hand. She had been crying and asking for Clara all evening. He was at his wit's end. Hopefully, a good night's sleep would put Lily in a better frame of mind.

"Clara isn't here, and if I don't braid your hair tonight it will be full of tangles in the morning." He held out his hand.

She threw the brush across the room. "I don't care. I want to see my friend. She said you would take me to her house to meet her dog and her sheep. Why can't we go there?"

He walked across the room and picked up the brush. "It's getting dark outside, and it's time for bed, Lily. Clara will be asleep soon, and so should you."

He sat down at the edge of her bed. "Let me finish your hair."

"I'll do it." She took the brush from him and managed to smooth most of the strands between her sniffles.

When she was done, he gently braided her soft blond locks and tied a ribbon on the end. It was a lopsided braid, but it was the best he could do.

She rubbed her red-rimmed and swollen eyes with the back of her fists. "Can I go see Clara tomorrow?"

"We'll talk about it in the morning." He covered

her with a light sheet. The truly surprising thing was how much he wanted to see Clara again, too.

"I miss her." Lily started crying and buried her face in the pillow.

Ethan sat beside her stroking her head until her sobs tapered off and eventually stopped. When she was asleep, he went downstairs and climbed wearily into his own bed.

It felt as if he'd only had his eyes closed for a minute when he felt someone patting his face. He opened one eye. Lily, with her braid undone and her hair in a mat of tangles, stood beside his bed. Only the faintest hint of light showed around the edge of the blind over his window. It wasn't even dawn yet.

"Can we go see Clara now?" Lily asked hopefully.

"*Nee,* we can't. Stop this nonsense."

Lily burst into tears and sobbed harder than she had yesterday.

He sat up. There wouldn't be any more sleep for him.

He tried to console her without success. Even her brothers couldn't distract her when they got up. Lily refused to eat her breakfast and sat hiccuping at the table. The boys kept casting worried glances in his direction.

What did he do now?

The answer was clear. He needed Clara.

* * *

Clara rose, dressed quietly so as not to wake anyone else and went downstairs to start breakfast.

The entire family had made plans to travel to Hope Springs that afternoon to visit with Naomi and her family and see the new baby. Clara looked forward to the trip. When it was almost time to leave, Clara went out to gather a few fresh sweet corn ears to take along as a gift. As she was gathering the corn, she heard a wagon approaching along the lane.

She came out of the corn patch with her armload of ears to see who it was just as an enormous pair of draft horses trotted past. She clamped her lips closed on a shriek and managed to stand still, although her arms trembled enough to make her drop a few ears.

When the wagon was past, she realized it was Ethan at the reins. He hadn't seen her. All the children were seated beside him. She followed the wagon to the house.

Her grandfather had come out to meet the visitors. "*Guter mariye.* Welcome to my home."

"Good morning. I've come to speak to your granddaughter."

Joe regarded the group on the wagon with a slight smile twitching at the corner of his mouth. "Which granddaughter? I have four."

"I wanna…see…Clara," Lily said with a catch in her voice. Was she crying?

Clara hurried around to the side of the wagon. "Lily, what's wrong?"

"Clara!" Lily threw herself off the wagon seat and into Clara's arms. Ears of corn flew everywhere as Clara caught her. Lily wrapped her arms tightly around Clara's neck and held on for dear life.

Greta, Betsy and Lizzie came out of the house to meet the visitors. They stood on each side of her grandfather. Clara wanted to send them all back inside, but she couldn't think of a reason to do so. There would be a wagonload of questions about this visit from a stranger and his children.

Ethan looked worn to the bone. "I can't get anything done! She's been like this since you left yesterday. She cried herself to sleep. She started crying the minute she woke up. Nothing I've tried will make her stop."

Lily's sobs were tapering off to hiccups. Clara cringed at Ethan's frustrated tone. She hadn't meant to make things harder for him. Now he had one more reason to be angry with her. "I'm so sorry."

Her grandfather moved to her side. "What has my granddaughter to do with your child's unhappiness?"

Her face burning, Clara held her breath as she waited for Ethan to tell everyone about her appalling behavior.

Chapter Four

Ethan watched the color drain from Clara's cheeks. She cast him an imploring look before she dropped her gaze.

Did she think he had come to chastise her in front of her family for spying on him? Far from it. He wasn't sure what to make of her behavior yesterday, but he needed her help.

He hoped he wasn't making a mistake.

"Mr. Shetler, your granddaughter came to my farm with Faith Lapp a few days ago to tell me my nephew Micah had been up to some mischief. Yesterday, she found my two youngest playing in the creek alone and brought them home. It seems the children are in need of a better caretaker than I have been. Lily, my niece, has taken a great liking to Clara. I've come to offer her a job."

Everyone looked at Clara. She didn't say anything, but she shot him a grateful glance before looking down again. She relaxed a little and pushed her hands into the pockets of her apron.

"My granddaughter has a job. She works for Faith Lapp," Joseph said.

"It's my understanding that Clara doesn't work there anymore."

Joseph turned to Clara. "Is this true?"

She nodded. The women in her family seemed surprised by the news.

"You aren't?"

"Why didn't you say something?"

"When did this happen?" they asked one after the other without giving her a chance to answer.

When they grew silent, Clara said, "We finished all the yarn yesterday. I thought I mentioned it last night. Maybe I didn't."

"There's a lot you haven't mentioned," the youngest of her sisters quipped with a sharp look in Ethan's direction.

Ethan climbed down from his wagon and approached Clara. She took a quick step back. He stopped where he was. "Perhaps we could discuss this in private?" he asked.

She glanced at her family and then nodded. She detached Lily from her neck and smiled at the child. "This is my sister Betsy. She will take you to meet some of our lambs. Would you like that?"

His niece looked uncertain. He prayed she

wouldn't start crying again. She sniffed once. "Can't you show them to me?"

Clara lowered the girl to the ground. "I must speak with your *onkel,* but I will join you in a little while. Okay?"

"Okay."

That was far easier than he had imagined. The young woman came forward and took Lily by the hand. "We have lots of sheep and some baby kittens, too. Would you like to see them?"

A smile lit Lily's face. "I love kittens." She took Betsy's hand and went willingly. Her brothers tagged along after them.

It was a relief to see Lily acting normal again. Clara had a wondrous effect on the child. Ethan glanced at her. She met his gaze briefly and nodded toward the side yard. "Come this way."

He followed her to a group of chairs arranged in a semicircle beneath the spreading branches of an elm tree. She took a seat in the shade. He sat in the chair beside her. She leaned away from him and crossed her arms tightly over her middle. "Thank you for not telling my family how I spied on you."

"A thing that is forgiven should not be mentioned again."

"I wasn't sure that you had forgiven me."

She was such a timid creature. She barely spoke loud enough for him to hear, but he didn't move closer. He didn't want to frighten her. It was amazing that she had found the courage to eavesdrop on him. It proved she would put the needs of a child above her own comfort. There was more to Clara Barkman than met the eye.

"Lily has been inconsolable since you left. I'm serious about the job offer. I need someone to look after the children while I'm working. I haven't been logging since my brother, Greg, and his wife died. I need to get back to work or I won't be able to feed my family. I can't take them with me. It's too dangerous to have them around chain saws and falling trees."

"I can understand your concern." She looked up then, and he was struck once more by how pretty she was.

Her skin was smooth and tanned by the sun. Her eyebrows arched like slender wings over her bright blue eyes. They gave her a slightly inquisitive look. He hadn't noticed before because she was always looking down. Her hair, neatly parted in the center and swept back beneath her white *kapp* was blond with reddish highlights that reminded him of his teams' shiny coats. It was easy to imagine her hair glistening in the sunlight, too. How long would it be if she let it down?

He had no business thinking such things about a maiden. Only God and a husband were allowed to gaze upon a woman's crowning glory.

He realized he was staring when she blushed and

dropped her gaze again. He hadn't come to gawk at her. He was here to convince her to accept his job offer. He couldn't handle the children alone. He was willing to admit that now. Clara might be the straw he was clutching for, but he was growing desperate.

"If you would consider the job, you should know I occasionally have to take work that's too far away for me to get home at night. In that case, you may stay with the children at my place, or if you'd rather, you can bring the children home with you. I can't pay you until I deliver a load of logs to the sawmill, but after that it will be a weekly wage. What do you think?"

"You wish to hire me as your *kinder heedah?*"

"*Ja,* as a caregiver for the children."

She tipped her head to the side. "I had not thought of taking such a job myself. I know many young Amish girls work for the *Englisch* as nannies or for other Amish families as mother's helpers."

Ethan said, "The job would include some housekeeping chores, too. If that's acceptable?"

"I'm not sure I can take the job although it's very kind of you to offer. I have applied for the teaching position at Walnut Creek school. The bishop and the school board will be interviewing candidates in a few weeks. If I am chosen, I will have a lot of preparations to make before school starts in September."

He hadn't considered that she might have another job lined up already. "Would you consider working for me until you know for sure the teaching position is yours? Even a few weeks will give me time to find someone else."

"I expect I owe you that much."

He shook his head. "You don't owe me anything."

"I had such unkind thoughts about you. It was wrong of me."

"And you have my forgiveness. Forget it. If you want the job, it's yours. If you need time to think it over, could you please decide before I have to pry Lily away today? I'm not sure I can take another day of tears."

She smiled at that. It was only the tiniest curve of her lips, but it showed a dimple in her right cheek. It reminded him of Jenny. She had deep dimples in both cheeks that appeared every time she smiled. She used to smile at him and make his heart leap, but her smiles were all for someone else now. He swallowed hard against the tightness in his throat.

"Don't you have a family member who could help with the children?" Clara asked.

It was his turn to stare at the ground. "Greg was my only sibling. I have two aunts, who live in the community where we grew up in Indiana. One is willing to take Lily. The other one is willing to take Amos. My aunts are in their sixties. Neither of them is willing to take all the children and keep them together. Since Micah will be in school, they think I should keep him. He has a reputation for being something of a troublemaker."

"Well earned, I'm sure. I can understand why you don't want to split them up. I can't imagine being separated from my sisters. It would be heart-breaking."

He was tempted to tell her about his childhood. That was odd. He never spoke of it. Instead, he said, "My brother and his wife would want them to stay together. I know that as sure as I'm sitting here. I took the children without a second thought, but I had no idea how difficult it was going to be."

"You are blessed to have them."

Her wistful tone gave him hope. "I know that I am, and I want to raise them as Greg and his Mary would have liked."

She nodded. "I will discuss your offer with my grandfather. If he agrees, I'll look after the children until I find out if the teaching job is mine or not."

"And if the school board chooses someone else?"

"Why don't we wait and see how it goes until then. Do you think Micah will object to having me there?"

"Micah objects to everything these days. He'll get over it."

"I don't wish to cause more trouble for the two of you."

"If you agree, there won't be any trouble at all." He hoped and prayed that would be the case, but with Micah, he never knew.

"I don't think you should take the job." Greta folded her arms over her chest.

Back inside the house, Clara and two of her sisters were seated at the kitchen table while their grandfather spoke to Ethan outside. Betsy was still down in the barn with the children.

"Why shouldn't I?" Clara glanced toward the door. What was Ethan telling her grandfather? She didn't think he would relate how she spied on him, but she hated not knowing.

Greta scowled as she shook her head. "There is something not right about him."

"You're imagining things," Lizzie said. "I didn't see anything wrong with him."

Greta straightened in her chair. "It was the way he looked at you, Clara."

"How did he look at me?" Had she missed something? So often her gaze was fastened to her shoes. It wasn't modesty. It was apprehension that kept her from looking life in the face. It seemed that she was always afraid.

Greta leaned her forearms on the table. "I don't know how to describe it. It was like he couldn't take his eyes off you. Besides, if you thought he was a nice fellow, why didn't you mention meeting him? Not once, but twice."

It was time to fess up. "I didn't say anything because after Faith and I took Micah home, I went back to spy on Ethan."

"Why?" Greta asked.

"To see if he was as cruel to Micah as our *onkel* was to us. I'm ashamed to admit that I eavesdropped outside his window. I was nearly discovered, but I hid under his porch like a scolded dog. It's not an easy thing to confess."

Lizzie began to giggle. "I would have given a lot to see that. You are always so proper, Clara. I can't imagine you crawling under a porch. You never did things like that even when we were children."

"With good reason. There was dirt and cobwebs. A lot of cobwebs. It is not something I intend to repeat." She was still embarrassed by the incident, but she could see how Lizzie found it amusing.

Lizzie folded her hands on the table. "I think you should take the job. I think taking care of his children for a few weeks is the perfect way to see if you are cut out to be a teacher."

Clara cocked her head to the side. "Why wouldn't I be cut out to be a teacher?"

"I'm not saying that you aren't. I'm just saying it is something you've never tried. It might be worse than crawling under a porch."

"I doubt that," Clara said as she suppressed a shudder.

Lizzie's grin widened. "It will give you a chance to find out if you like taking care of children before you commit to doing it for a year."

"You seem to forget that I took care of all of you for years. Especially Betsy."

Lizzie shrugged. "Taking care of younger sisters is a far cry from taking care of a whole school."

Greta shook her head. "I still think it's a bad idea. We don't know Ethan Gingerich. He hasn't been in this community for long, and he isn't a member of our church. I just think it's a bad idea."

Lizzie brushed aside her objections with a wave of her hand. "We haven't been here long, but we were welcomed with open arms. We should not do less."

"I haven't made up my mind," Clara admitted.

Lizzie rose to her feet. "You should pray about it. In the meantime, we have a supper to finish putting together. Those baskets won't pack themselves."

Her sisters stood and went about preparing for an afternoon of visiting, but Clara remained seated at the table. What should she do?

Ethan endured Joe Shetler's scrutiny without flinching. He knew his request was an unusual one. As a single man, having Clara, a young single woman, working in his home might be frowned upon by some.

Joe pushed the brim of his straw hat a little higher. "I've heard that you are a logger."

Ethan nodded. "I am. I have worked for a few of your neighbors. I can give you their names and you can ask them about me."

"I have a stand of old walnut trees that could use thinning, but it's up above the lake. The ground is steep in places."

"My teams can work just about anywhere that a horse can stand. I'd be happy to take a look at your trees and see if it's feasible to log some of them out. Old-growth walnut brings a nice price at the sawmill. The cabinetmakers love it."

"I might have you do that. Where are your people from?"

This was more along the line of questioning that Ethan expected. "My family hails from southern Indiana. I moved here two years ago. I bought a place out on Cherry Creek Road."

"Do you still have family in Indiana?"

"Two maiden aunts, who think I should be married and bring it up every chance they get." He didn't mention his estranged mother, who still lived there. Some things were best left in the past. "I came here looking for a little peace and quiet. You know how women can be."

Joe chuckled and jerked his head toward the

house. “I had thirty years of peace and quiet, but that has gone by the wayside. I have four granddaughters and a new wife in my house.”

“My condolences.”

Joe gave a sharp bark of laughter and slapped Ethan’s shoulder. “That’s a good one. Most people offer their congratulations.”

“I reckon it’s all in how a man looks at things.” He glanced toward the house. Had Clara come to a decision? If she said no, he would have to find someone else. Maybe she could recommend someone. Oddly, he didn’t want anyone else but her.

He was unfamiliar with the single young women of the area who might be looking for work. He avoided socializing, avoided the singings and picnics where the young people gathered because he had no plans to start courting again. He couldn’t imagine giving his heart, or what was left of it, to another woman. The cost was too dear when love wasn’t returned.

The sound of voices drew his attention to the barn, where he saw Clara’s sister coming out with the children.

Joe glanced that way, too. “I’d say your days of peace and quiet are over if you have three young’uns to care for.”

“They are my brother’s children. He and his wife were struck by lightning while they were out in the field." Ethan's throat closed tight. He blinked hard and swallowed back his sorrow.

Joe's eyes softened with pity. "I'm sorry to hear that. It's a rare thing, but I've known it to happen. God wanted them both with Him. We cannot understand His ways. We can only trust in His love. I can see why you need a hand with the children."

"I'll manage, but it would be much easier if I had someone to look after them while I'm working. I don't like the idea of having them with me while I'm felling trees. Things can go wrong in a heartbeat."

Lily raced up to him. "*Onkel* Ethan, they have sheeps. Lots and lots of sheeps. I petted a baby one."

He swung her up into his arms. "Did you now?"

"Uh-huh, I did."

"So did I," Amos added, hopping beside Ethan. "Betsy and her sisters are from Indiana just like we are. They all came here on a big bus, not a little van like we rode in. Did you know we can go to Indiana on a bus?"

"I did know that. Perhaps we will go back there someday."

"Soon?" Micah asked, looking hopeful.

Ethan shook his head. Lily cupped her hands on Ethan's cheeks to make sure he was looking at her. "Can we take a lamb home, please?"

Micah strolled up to the group with much less

enthusiasm. He hooked his thumbs in his suspenders. "They weren't anything special. They're just dumb animals."

Amos looked from Micah's set face to the ground and then ran his thumbs beneath his suspenders in imitation of his brother. "Yeah, they're just dumb animals. We don't want one, Lily."

She threw her brothers a disgusted look. "I want one, and *Onkel* Ethan is going to buy one for me."

Joe chuckled. "I'm sorry, but I don't have any lambs for sale today."

Her bottom lip quivered. "Not even one?"

"*Nee,* not even one."

She sighed. "That makes me sad."

Joe exchanged glances with Ethan and managed to keep a straight face. "Ach, it makes me sad to see you sad, little one. My wife made some pretty *goot* banana bread yesterday. Would a slice of that make you feel better?"

Ethan struggled not to laugh as Lily solemnly considered Joe's offer. She finally nodded. "I think it might."

"*Goot.* I think it will make me feel better, too." Joe held his hand toward her.

She wiggled down from Ethan's arms, took Joe's hand and said, "Come on, Amos." Together they all went into the house.

"Can't we go home now?" Micah asked.

"Without your brother and sister? Why don't you go in and have some bread, too."

"I'm not hungry, and they can eat their bread on the way home."

"We will go when Clara has given me an answer."

"An answer to what?"

"I offered her a job taking care of you children."

"I don't need a babysitter."

"It's not a decision that is up to you." Ethan didn't feel like arguing with the boy.

"I don't want her watching me all the time. I can take care of Amos and Lily. We don't need her."

Ethan understood Micah's need to be the man of the family and take care of his younger brother and sister. "I know you think you can."

"Why do we need her? You said you'd take care of us. Why aren't you taking care of us?"

"I'm doing the best I can, Micah, but I've got to earn a living and that means logging. It's too dangerous to take you *kinder* with me. If Clara accepts the job, I can work and not worry about the three of you."

He heard the door open, and Clara came out of the house. She stood on the porch looking nervous and uncertain. Micah made a disgusted face. Ethan walked up to the foot of the steps and waited for her to speak. She seemed to have trouble finding her voice. Finally, he asked, “Have you made up your mind?”

“I have. I’ve talked it over with Grandfather, and he has left the decision up to me.”

Ethan waited impatiently for her answer. He couldn’t read her face. “What have you decided?”

Chapter Five

Now that she faced Ethan, Clara had second thoughts about her decision. There was something about him that left her feeling…breathless. It was a new sensation. No man had ever affected her this way. She crossed her arms tightly to suppress the excitement he caused.

Maybe it was the way he studied her face. As though he were intent on catching her every expression. She wasn't used to such scrutiny. She preferred to go unnoticed. The urge to scurry back in the house grew stronger. Was Greta right? Was she about to make a mistake?

He shifted from one foot to the other as he waited for her reply. He was a man who found it hard to stand still, but he didn't pressure her. It helped her make up her mind.

"I have decided to accept your job offer. I'll watch the children until I hear from the school board." She was doing it for the children. Because they needed her. It surprised her just how much she wanted to be needed.

How pathetic was that?

Micah came to stand beside Ethan. He rolled his eyes. "Oh, that's just great."

Ethan cupped an arm around Micah's shoulders and pulled him close. "*Ja,* it's *wunderbar!*"

Clara bit her lip to keep from smiling. Ethan's grin was forced, but she read pure relief in his eyes.

"How soon can you start?" he asked.

"Bright and early tomorrow morning."

"*Goot.* I have customers who have been waiting on me to cut their trees. I'll let them know that I can start right away. *Danki.*"

Amos and Lily came out of the house. They each held a thick slice of banana bread in their hands. Ethan called them. "Come get in the wagon."

Lily stopped beside Clara and leaned against her leg. "But I don't want to go home."

Clara stooped to her level and lifted the child's chin to face her. "You must do as your *onkel* says without making a fuss, for God values a quiet spirit."

Lily whispered, "Will you come home with me?"

"Not today, but I will see you tomorrow. You and I will have lots of time to spend together. Now be a *goot* girl, and do as your *onkel* bids."

"Okay." Lily ran to Ethan. He helped her into the wagon and climbed up after her. The boys climbed in the back unaided. Ethan tipped his hat to Clara and turned his team around. With a click of his tongue, he sent the big horses trotting smartly down the lane.

Her grandfather came and stood behind her. Her sisters crowded around. "Are you sure you want to do this?" Greta asked.

Clara nodded. "I don't see the harm in it."

Betsy shot her a skeptical look. "You don't? The children may get too attached to you. They're very young."

"I will make sure that they understand it's only for a short while. Are we ready to go to town? I am anxious to meet Naomi's new grandbaby."

"As am I," their grandfather declared. "It's been a long time since I've held a *bobli.* I'm afraid I'm out of practice."

Betsy giggled. "How can you say that? You care for and bottle-feed tiny lambs every spring. I think you've had more practice with babies than most men."

"I don't think lambs count. Come, girls, and get a move on. If I know Naomi, she will have a fine meal waiting for us."

They all rushed back into the house to get ready, but Clara stayed on the porch watching Ethan's wagon as it disappeared down the lane. Had she done the right thing? She would be seeing him on a daily basis. Why did the idea excite her?

* * *

Ethan kept his horses at a steady trot. The empty wagon was easy for them to pull, and they hadn't had much exercise the past few weeks. That was all going to change now. A huge weight had been lifted from him by Clara's decision. He couldn't believe she had accepted his offer. He was even more surprised that her family had agreed to let her work for a bachelor. He would take care to see that her reputation was protected, but in truth, his three children would be adequate chaperones.

Lily, who had been crying for two days, sat beside him quietly with her hands folded in her lap. He looked down at her. "Are you happy that Clara will be taking care of you?"

"I'm very happy," she said softly.

"You're being awfully quiet about it."

"That's because Clara told me that God loves a quiet spirit. Clara has a quiet spirit. I think that God loves her."

"God loves all of His children, Lily."

She glanced over her shoulder and leaned closer to him. "Even Micah?"

He nodded solemnly. "*Ja,* even Micah."

"But I don't think he has a quiet spirit."

"He will have one when he is older."

"When he is old like you? Do you have a quiet spirit, *Onkel* Ethan?"

Did he? The child's question caught him by surprise. It had been a long time since he had examined his relationship with God. He said his prayers, he attended church as an Amish man was required to do, but he no longer trusted that God would take care of him.

"I reckon its quiet enough," he said, but it wasn't the whole truth. His spirit had become more resentful than quiet. The events of his life, the betrayal by people he loved, had made him doubt God's goodness, made him feel that God had turned away from him, too. Why didn't he deserve the love others found so easily?

There was no point dwelling on a question with no answer. He'd come to Hope Springs intending to start a new life. He looked down at the little girl beside him. This was a new life all right, but not one he expected.

Lily wrapped her arms around his arm and hugged him tight. "I miss *Mamm* and *Daed,* but I'm glad that you came to take care of us."

"I'm glad that I did, too."

He *was* glad to have the children in his life. He prayed it was God's plan for them to remain with him for good. He prayed, too, that he would grow to love them as every child deserved to be loved. Unconditionally.

The eastern sky was glowing bright gold beyond the trees at the top of the ridge, but the sun wasn't yet up when Ethan returned to the house after doing his morning chores and checking his logging equipment. He stopped at the woodpile to gather an armload for the kitchen stove and glanced down the lane. When would Clara arrive? He wanted to start as soon as possible and get most of his work done before the heat of the afternoon. There was no sign of her so he walked into the house and stopped short.

She was already busy at the stove. The smell of frying bacon filled the air. The children sat at the kitchen table looking at her like starving puppies. Puppies with freshly scrubbed faces and neatly combed hair.

"Good morning," she said softly but kept her back to him.

He dropped the load of wood into the box by the stove. "Good morning. When you said bright and early you meant it. I didn't see your buggy outside. Did someone bring you?"

"I walked. I like walking. I knew you would want to get started early. Breakfast is almost ready."

"You don't need to fix anything for me. I'll be working over at Elam Sutter's place. Do you know it?"

She turned away from the stove and wiped her hands on her apron. "I do. My sister Betsy works in his basket-weaving shop."

"*Goot.* You can find me there if you should need

me. I'll be home about six o'clock." He took his hat from a peg by the door and put it on.

"Don't you want some breakfast?" She carried a plate piled high with biscuits to the table.

"*Nee,* the coffee I had earlier is enough for me."

"What about lunch? Shall I make you something now, or should I bring it by later?"

"Elam's wife is feeding me, so you don't need to worry about that. Just look after the children. That's all I need."

She glanced around the kitchen. "Is it all right if I clean up?"

He looked around and didn't see anything wrong. "Clean up what?"

"The floor could use a scrubbing." She returned to the stove and loaded a plate with bacon.

He glanced down at his floor. "I swept it yesterday."

"Yes, but when was the last time you washed it?"

"I haven't seen him wash it since I've been here," Amos said, reaching for the bacon.

Leave it to the *kinder* to make him look bad.

Clara moved the bacon beyond the boy's reach. "We don't eat until after we give thanks, Amos."

"Sorry. I forgot. It sure smells good. *Onkel* Ethan burns the bacon when he cooks it." Amos folded his hands and tried to look virtuous.

"Clean as you see fit, but I don't expect you to keep house for us." The bacon did smell good.

Ethan's stomach rumbled loud enough for Clara to hear. A grin twitched at the corner of her lips.

"Are you sure you don't want a little something to eat? Work is twice as hard on an empty stomach."

"Maybe just a little bacon and a biscuit." He hung his hat back on the peg and took a seat at the head of the table.

"I can scramble you a few eggs. It won't take any time at all."

"Are you sure? I don't want to make more work for you."

"Nothing is easier than scrambling eggs. Go ahead and start with what's on the table."

"Will you join us?"

"I ate before I came this morning."

"All right." He bowed his head and silently prayed the blessing before meals and the Lord's Prayer. When he was finished, he cleared his throat to signal the children that he was done. Taking some bacon, he forked some onto Lily's plate and then handed it to Micah. Micah all but emptied the plate and then handed it to Amos. There was only one strip of bacon left.

"Hey, I need more than this. Give me some of yours, Micah."

Micah popped a piece into his mouth. "I'm older than you. I get more."

"That doesn't matter." Amos scowled at his brother.

"You can have some of mine," Lily said. She pushed her plate toward him.

Ethan was listening to the children with only half an ear. His attention was on Clara. Her movements were graceful and deliberate without any waste of energy. Her presence, which he thought would make him uncomfortable, was having the opposite effect. There was something calming about her.

She turned around, came to the table and took Micah's plate from him.

He frowned. "Hey, what are you doing? I wasn't finished."

"I am older than you are so I get more."

"But you said you weren't going to eat." Micah's frown turned to an angry pout. They both looked at Ethan.

He could tell by the look on Clara's face that he was supposed to deal with this. He should've skipped breakfast. He could be happily harnessing his horses right this minute.

"Micah, share with your brother." He took a bite of biscuit.

Clara didn't move. She still held Micah's plate, but her gaze was fixed on Ethan. He swallowed what he had in his mouth, returned his partially eaten biscuit to his plate and folded his hands. Apparently, he needed to expound on the issue. "No one deserves more because they are older or because they are bigger, Micah. We are all equal in the sight of God. We must share what we have with those who have less."

Clara smiled and Ethan took a relieved breath. She said, "In this way, Micah, we please God and we take care of each other."

"I don't care if I please God. I'm not hungry, anyway." Micah jumped up from the table and ran upstairs.

Ethan sighed deeply. "What did I say that was wrong?"

Clara was surprised that Ethan didn't put the blame on her. Surprised, but pleased at how willing he was to accept responsibility and advice. Advice she didn't have at present. She put Micah's plate back on the table and gave two pieces of his bacon to Amos. "I don't think we said anything wrong. Micah can't always get his way. He must learn that his choices have consequences. He will come down when he is hungry."

"I'm sorry he acted this way on your first day with us. I will go talk to him if you think I should."

"*Nee,* you have work to do. I will deal with the children."

"Are you sure?"

"Ja."

Relief brightened his eyes. He rose to his feet, tucked a biscuit in his pocket and took his hat from the peg. "Clara is in charge while I am gone. You will obey her."

"But I am being good," Lily said, her eyes wide.

"Me, too," Amos chimed in.

Ethan's smile crinkled the corners of his eyes. Clara was struck by what a nice smile he had. "You are being good. See that you stay that way."

She said, "Finish your breakfast, children. Might I have a word with you outside, Ethan?"

He frowned slightly but nodded. He held open the door and she walked out onto the porch with him. "Before you go, I wanted to ask what chores the children have. What are their responsibilities?"

His frown deepened. "To stay out of trouble and out from underfoot. If you think of something that you want them to do, just tell them. Do what you think is best."

That was odd. They were all old enough to have simple chores. "What type of discipline would you expect me to carry out?" she asked.

"Do what you think is best," he said again in irritation.

"Very well. I thought it was important that we discuss these things."

"And we have. I've got to get going. Is there anything else?"

She thought of a dozen things to ask but kept silent, reluctant to upset him. She fastened her gaze to the porch floor. "Have a good day."

He didn't leave. He stood where he was until she looked up. "I'm sorry if I sounded short with you. I appreciate your help with the children, Clara. I trust that you can handle anything that comes up. If you think they need chores to do, we'll discuss it when I get back this evening."

Inordinately pleased by his confidence, she nodded mutely. He turned and strode toward the barn. She went back in the house and started to clean up. The window over the sink was open to catch the morning breeze. A few minutes later, Ethan and his team went thundering past as they headed up the drive.

Clara couldn't suppress a shudder at the sound of their powerful hooves striking the ground. It reminded her of the blows she had suffered at the hands of her uncle and the man he tried to force her to marry. Her hands grew cold as she clenched them together. She squeezed her eyes shut.

"I wanna help wash the dishes. Can I?"

Clara opened her eyes and saw Lily gazing at her. The past was over and done with. While it haunted her, it could no longer hurt her. She must live in the present. Her uncle had robbed her and her sisters of ten long years, forcing them to live in drudgery and fear. He couldn't have one more minute of her life.

Drawing a deep breath, Clara smiled at the girl. "Of course you may. Why don't you get a chair so you can stand beside me. I will wash and you can rinse. How does that sound?"

"Like fun!" Lily hopped up and down and dashed to the table.

"What can I do?" Amos asked, looking uncertain.

"Do you have any chores?"

"Micah and I have to pick up our room and make our beds when *Onkel* Ethan tells us."

"That's *goot,* but we will not wait for him to tell us. We will do it every day and surprise him."

"Okay."

"For now, why don't you take a broom and sweep the front porch and steps."

"Why?"

"So they are clean and neat."

"Why?" he asked again.

"Because when God has given us a fine place to live, we must take care of it. We must be good stewards of the land and all we own."

"Is it woman's work? Micah says we boys don't do woman's work."

She folded her arms over her chest. "Is that what Micah says?"

"Yup," Amos and Lily answered together. Clara helped the little girl climb onto the chair beside her at the sink.

"Is it woman's work to cook?" she asked.

"Sure." Amos nodded once.

"Who has done the cooking since you came here?"

"*Onkel* Ethan," Lily said.

"Is laundry woman's work?" Clara asked Amos.

"I think so," he said slowly.

"Who has been doing your laundry?"

"*Onkel* Ethan."

She thought he was beginning to see her point. "Is planting the crops and taking care of them men's work?"

"*Ja!* That's men's work." He looked pleased that he knew this answer.

"And have you ever seen women working in the fields?"

"Sometimes." His expression grew puzzled.

"That's right. A woman must know how to drive a team and till the soil when needed. Just as a man must know how to cook and clean clothes when there is no one else to do it for him. Do you understand?"

"I guess. It means I have to sweep the porch. I know where the broom is." He collected it from a closet beside the refrigerator, pulled his straw hat off one of the lower pegs by the front door and went out.

Lily, waiting quietly on the chair beside Clara, asked, "Can I drive *Onkel* Ethan's team? I love his horses."

"Oh, no!" Clara said quickly. Lily's eyes widened.

Clara realized her mistake immediately. She

didn't want to pass on her fear of draft horses to the child. "I mean, maybe when you are older, but you must not go near them unless you are with your *onkel.* They can hurt you very badly."

"*Onkel* says I must talk or sing when I am near them and never run behind them so they don't get scared."

The animals were as big as houses. What did they have to be afraid of? "You must always do as he says. Promise?"

"Okay. Are you going to wash those dishes?"

"*Ja,* and then we will scrub the floors." Clara glanced out the window to see where Amos was and then set to work. She would prove to Ethan that his faith in her wasn't misplaced.

Three hours later, with the kitchen spotless and the younger children playing with a puzzle in the living room, she pulled two fresh loaves of bread from the oven. She had used the last of the day-old bread to make bread pudding and meat loaf for supper. It would soon be too hot to cook in the kitchen. She glanced up the stairs in concern. Micah still hadn't come down. He had to be hungry by now.

"That sure smells *goot.*" Amos came into the room with a hopeful expression.

"Would you like a slice of hot bread?"

His eyes brightened. "With church spread on it? That's how *Mamm* used to fix it."

She dumped the loaves on the counter and wiped

the sweat from her brow with her sleeve. "Yum. Peanut butter and marshmallow crème all melted and gooey on fresh hot bread. That sounds perfect. Why don't you go tell Micah to come down and we'll all have some."

Amos darted for the stairs. "Micah! We're having church spread on hot bread!"

Clara smiled at his enthusiasm. She sliced the bread, put it on plates and began mixing the ingredients for the treat. Lily came in and climbed onto her chair. She propped her chin in her hands.

"What's the matter, Lily? Don't you like church spread?"

"I do, but this is going to make more dirty dishes to wash."

Clara laughed out loud. "I will do them."

Amos came tromping down the stairs and took his seat at the table.

"Is Micah coming?" Clara asked.

"*Nee,* he's not in our room."

Clara frowned. "Where is he?"

Amos shrugged and reached for a slice of bread.

Annoyed, Clara decided to check for herself. Micah wasn't happy to have her looking after him, but he wasn't going to be able to hide all day.

His room was empty. She dropped to her knees, feeling foolish, and looked under the bed. He wasn't there, either. She sat back on her heels. Where could he be?

Quickly, she checked the other rooms. Nothing. She searched the house from top to bottom calling his name. She even searched the cellar. If he was in the building, she couldn't find him.

Walking out onto the front porch, she scanned the yard and tried to calm her rising sense of panic as the other children came to stand beside her.

Lily tugged on Clara's apron. "Is Micah lost?"

She smiled to reassure the child. "I think he's playing hide-and-seek."

Lily cupped her hands around her mouth and yelled, *"Alle alle achts und frei."*

When Micah didn't appear, Lily shook her head. "I think he's lost."

Amos shoved his hands in his pockets. "*Onkel* Ethan isn't gonna be happy."

"I want you and Lily to go in and finish your snack." The children went inside, and Clara quickly knelt beside the lattice to peek under the porch. Micah wasn't there.

What did she do now? Ethan's confidence in her ability to manage anything was sadly misplaced. Should she gather the neighbors to help her look for the boy? What if he wasn't hiding from her as she suspected? What if he was hurt and couldn't call for help.

Had he gone in with the horses?

Panic sent her heart pounding at the thought. She

would have to check their stalls. Cold sweat beaded on her forehead. "Please, Lord, help me do this."

She rose to her feet and started toward the barn.

Chapter Six

Clara trembled so hard she could barely open the barn door. Inside, she stood frozen in place when Ethan's mares hung their heads over their stall doors and looked her way. She couldn't hear anything but the hammering of her own heart.

She had to make sure Micah wasn't lying injured in one of those stalls. Her own fear of the big horses made her imagine the worst. She raised her gaze upward to pray for courage and caught a glimpse of a straw hat in the hayloft opening above her. "Micah?"

The wearer of the hat jerked back out of her line of sight.

Relief was quickly followed by vexation. He wasn't hurt. He wasn't lost. He was making a fool out of her. She was done with this game. "Micah, come down here this minute."

He didn't. She climbed the steep wooden stairs

to the loft, but didn't see him. There were dozens of places to hide. She walked toward the large open doorway at the back of the barn, staying well away from the edge. She didn't care for heights. A ladder to the ground stood propped in the opening. Clara shaded her eyes and scanned the fields. She saw Micah running toward the creek. She returned to the stairs and left the barn. She would find him if she had to search every inch of the farm, and then they would have a serious talk.

Much later that afternoon, Clara stood on the porch of Ethan's house ringing her hands as she watched him driving his team up the lane. How was she going to tell him that Micah was missing? Ethan was counting on her to care for his children, but she had failed miserably.

Her stomach twisted in knots.

"There's Micah," Amos shouted.

She looked to see where the child was pointing and saw Micah walking out of the barn. She raced toward him with the other children right behind her. She fell to her knees and grasped his shoulders.

"Where have you been? Didn't you hear us calling for you?" she demanded.

"I was playing in the barn." He wouldn't meet her gaze.

Lily put her arm around his waist. "I thought you was lost forever."

"Sorry, sis." At least he seemed to regret upsetting his sister.

"That's okay," Lily said kindly.

Clara didn't feel as forgiving. She rose to her feet. "In the future, please don't disappear without telling someone where you are going. Is that understood?"

He glared at her from beneath his lowered brow. "Are you going to tell *Onkel* Ethan?"

"Tell him what? That you were playing in the barn. I see no reason to mention it." No reason to mention she had been tearing her hair out for hours while the child made a fool of her? No, she wasn't about to tell Ethan that.

Micah was a troubled boy, more troubled than she had suspected. It would take time for him to trust her. Sadly, time was something she might not have to give him. She would learn of the school board's decision in a few weeks. If they hired her, Ethan would have to find someone else to care for the children. Someone who could do a better job than she had done.

Ethan drove his team into the farmyard. Clara and the children were all gathered in front of the barn. They had been on his mind all day. It was surprising how good it felt to see them waiting for him. He pulled his tired horses to a stop and smiled at Clara. "I see you survived the day. How was it?"

"Fine. It was a fine day," she said quickly.

Something in her tone caused him to doubt that statement. He noticed her *kapp* was askew, with yellow bits of straw or something sticking to it. Her apron was wrinkled. There was a smear of dirt on her cheek and smudges on her dress as if she'd been kneeling on the ground.

He got down from his logging arch. Lily came running up to him. He lifted her into his arms and walked toward Clara and the boys. Micah wore his mulish expression that spelled trouble. What was up?

Ethan looked at Lily, who seemed truly glad he was home. "What did you do all day while I was gone?"

"I helped Clara wash the dishes and the kitchen floor and I put a puzzle together with Amos and then we looked and looked for Micah."

Clara's face turned bright pink. Micah stared at his toes.

"More hide-and-seek?" Ethan asked Clara.

"Something like that," she said, and bit her lower lip.

"Shouldn't you go home," Micah suggested with a sharp glance in her direction.

Her eyes narrowed as she glared back at him. "I will. After I've had a chance to talk to your *onkel*."

Ethan set Lily on the ground. His hope that Clara had enjoyed an uneventful day vanished. "Micah, take the children up to the house. I'll be in after I put the team away. Clara, you and I can talk while I finish with them."

Micah didn't look pleased, but he took each of his siblings by the hand and went to the house. Ethan went to the front of his team and began unhitching them. Clara stood off to the side. Freeing Dutch first, and then Fred, he led them to the corral gate and tied them up. He began unbuckling Dutch's harness. "So? How did it go? Don't tell me that it went fine, because you and Micah both looked ready to spit nails."

"We had a misunderstanding, but I think we have sorted it out. Amos and Lily were no trouble at all."

"Would you care to tell me what your misunderstanding with Micah was about?"

"Not really. Micah doesn't know me. He has no reason to trust me, but I want to show him I'm a trustworthy person. You did tell me to do what I thought was best."

Surprised by the hint of defiance in her tone, he shrugged. She had a point. He pulled the heavy harness off Dutch and tossed it on the top rail of the fence. Dutch shook all over, snorted and tried to rub his headstall off using the fence. Clara jumped back three feet.

"Stop that." Ethan pushed the horse's head away from the boards.

"I'm sorry. I can't help it," Clara said quickly.

He glanced her way. She thought he was scolding her? He had forgotten that she was afraid of his animals. "I was talking to the horse, Clara. Not to you."

"Oh." She fell silent but didn't move closer.

After untying Dutch, Ethan opened the corral gate and turned him loose inside. The big horse ambled to the center of the pen. He put his nose to the ground and turned around several times before dropping to his knees and then rolling onto his side. After rocking a few times, Dutch managed to turn onto his back, where he proceeded to squirm and twist, scratching his back in the dirt with his big feet flailing in the air.

Ethan began unbuckling Fred's harness. He glanced at Clara. "Will you be back tomorrow?"

"If you wish me to come, I'll be here."

Ethan turned Fred in with Dutch. Like his teammate, Fred found a spot, turned in circles and lay down to scratch his back, too. Ethan turned to Clara. "I would like you to come back. What was it that you wanted to speak to me about?"

"You said this morning that we would discuss the children's chores when you came home. Have you decided what you want them to do?"

He'd forgotten all about it. "They've only been here a few weeks. I wanted to let them settle in before putting them to work."

"Having work to do will help them settle in

faster. Having nothing to do gives them far too much idle time. A bored child will get into trouble much faster than a busy one."

"They're little. What could they do?" He found himself on the defensive. He didn't like the feeling.

"Lots of things. They can feed and water the chickens. They can gather the eggs. They can clean the stalls. The lawn needs to be mowed. They can help with the upkeep of the house and the garden. Children should know they're contributing to the welfare of the family." She pointed to the corral. "Your fence needs painting. Micah and Amos are old enough to do that.

Ethan shifted uncomfortably. "They might not do a good job."

"Not as good as you perhaps, but they could do well enough."

"And if I have to come along and redo it, they will feel bad."

Clara tipped her head slightly as she regarded him. "You're afraid of hurting their feelings?"

"These children have been through a lot. They don't need to try and please me."

"Children want to please their parents."

"That's just it. I'm not their parent. I can't replace their father. No one can replace my brother. He was the best man I ever knew. It's been a long day and I'm tired. Give the children whatever chores you see fit. I'll hitch Rosie to the wagon and take you home."

"I'd rather walk."

"Suit yourself." He brushed past her and strode toward the house. A glance back showed she was on her way down the lane. At least she had said she was coming back tomorrow.

Inside, Micah was standing by the kitchen table with his fists clenched at his sides. "What did she tell you?"

Ethan wasn't ready to deal with the boy. He was struggling to keep a lid on his own emotions. He'd been rude to Clara. "We'll talk about it later, Micah."

"She's lying. I didn't hide from her all day."

So that was it. He leveled a stern gaze at his nephew. "Shame on you for calling that kind woman a liar. She never mentioned anything about you hiding from her."

Micah's mouth fell open. "She didn't?"

"*Nee,* she did not. Do you wish to tell me about this?"

Micah quickly shook his head.

"I thought not. Set the table for supper. I'll see what I can fix." Ethan was too tired to eat, but he knew he had to feed the children.

"Amos said Clara left a meat loaf and some vegetables in the refrigerator for us. All you need to do is warm it up." Micah began getting the plates down.

Ethan pulled open the refrigerator door. There was a generous meat loaf surrounded by mashed potatoes and carrots. On the shelf below was a pan of bread pudding studded with raisins. Much of the tension ebbed out of his body. "I think I'll have to give Clara a raise if I ever earn enough to pay her."

On the walk home, Clara had plenty of time to analyze her conversation with Ethan. It was amazing how quickly he had been transformed in her mind from someone big and frightening to someone she was concerned about. Someone who needed care and attention as much as the children did.

She was sure she saw more than Ethan wanted her to see. Micah wasn't the only one deeply troubled by the loss the family had suffered. Ethan was hurting, too. Unless he faced it and found a way to deal with his brother's death and accept that he was a parent to the children now, he couldn't help Micah. How could she help them both?

Ethan wouldn't welcome any interference on her part. She was sure of that. She would have to be careful. She would have to earn Ethan's trust the same way she was trying to earn Micah's. By being a friend.

It was late by the time she reached home. Her sisters were standing on the porch. Her grandfather and his hired man, Carl King, were walking up from the sheep pens. Carl's black-and-white English shepherd raced toward Clara the moment he caught sight of her. She stooped to pet the dog before continuing to the house.

"Well?" Greta demanded.

"Well what?" Clara replied, knowing full well what her sister meant.

"How did it go?" Betsy asked.

Clara sighed as she stared up at their curious faces. "It went."

"That bad?" Carl asked with a chuckle.

"Laugh if you want, but Micah Gingerich is a handful. Taking care of children is much more exhausting than spinning."

Lizzie came down the steps and linked her arm with Clara's. "You must be all done in. Come inside and sit down."

"You look like you could use a glass of iced tea before supper," Betsy added.

Clara nodded. "You read my mind, little sister."

"Tomorrow, you will take the pony and cart I bought for you to use," her grandfather said gruffly.

"You know I don't like to drive, *Daadi*."

"Then I will drive you and pick you up," he replied.

She could see that she would have little choice in the matter. "Very well, I will take the pony and cart. But if that animal runs away with me, I'm going to blame you."

Lizzie, Greta and Betsy all laughed. Betsy said,

"If you can get that fat little pony to run, I will eat my bonnet."

"Buttercup isn't fat," Greta said in the pony's defense. They all went into the house.

"What would you call it?" Carl asked.

"He's simply a little plump from not getting enough exercise. Clara, you'll be doing him a favor by driving him every day. One of us will harness him for you."

Clara went into the living room and sank gratefully onto the sofa. "I appreciate the offer, Greta, but I need to do it. My fear will not go away if I hide from it."

Lizzie sat on the other side of the sofa. Carl perched on the arm beside her. He said, "That is very true. The more you hide from a fear the larger it becomes. You know I speak from experience when I say that."

Clara nodded. Carl King looked like any other Amish man now, but Clara knew that until a few months ago, he had lived as an outsider, shunned and hiding from those who loved him, haunted by a terrible tragedy in his past. He had killed a man. Although he did so in self-defense, and to save the life of a young girl, he couldn't forgive himself. God had used the love of her sister Lizzie to bring Carl back to his faith and to a life without fear and shame. Being afraid of horses seemed like a small thing compared to what he had suffered.

Betsy came in with a glass of tea and handed it to Clara. "Supper will be ready in a minute."

Everyone except Clara and Greta got up and headed toward the kitchen. Clara took a long drink from her glass. Greta asked, "Are you sorry you took the job?"

Was she? In some ways. "It makes me think I'm not prepared to manage a whole school full of children."

"What is Ethan Gingerich like?"

Clara took another sip of her tea as she tried to form an answer. "He is a man struggling with an unexpected burden. No, *burden* is the wrong word. He doesn't see the children as a burden."

"That's good. I think children are sometimes a trial, but they should never be seen as a burden."

Clara rolled her eyes. "You did not spend hours looking for a boy who did not want to be found only to have him pop up two minutes before his *onkel* returned. *Ja,* Micah is a trial."

"You were worried about them, weren't you? Because they had been sent to live with their *onkel* the way we were."

"I know it was wrong of me to imagine Ethan was the same kind of man, yet when I first met him, I could not shake the fear that the children were being harmed. Ethan is not like that at all. I think he is grieving for the loss of his brother but trying to hide it from the children. He doesn't believe he can take his brother's place in their lives."

"You sound very taken with him."

Clara looked at her sister in surprise. "Do I? I'm not. I mean, I barely know the man."

"But?" Greta leaned closer.

"But what?"

"You barely know the man, but…?"

"But I feel sorry for him. The children, particularly Micah, are desperate for love and a sense of security that Ethan doesn't seem to be able to give them."

"And you think you can?"

"Of course I can't. I may only be with them for a couple of weeks."

"It takes less time than that for lonely children to fall in love with you and depend on you."

Greta was right. "When did you become such an expert on children?"

Greta blushed and looked away. Her sudden change of attitude triggered Clara's curiosity. "Is there something that you haven't been telling us?"

"I've been reading, that's all."

"Reading what, Greta?"

"I've been reading about abused children and how they are being helped by *Englisch* counselors and medicine," she said in a rush.

Clara took her sister's hand. "There is nothing to be ashamed of in that."

"I don't want to feel like a victim anymore. I want to do something positive. I want to help others, children and women like us. Is that prideful?"

"*Nee,* I don't think it is prideful at all. If that is where you believe God is leading you, then you must listen to His will, but do not confuse it with your own desires."

"I'll do my best."

"I don't doubt that for a minute."

"If I wanted to become a counselor, it would mean more schooling. It would mean I would have to leave the Amish."

Clara bit her lower lip. It would mean her beloved sister would move away from them. "Have you talked to anyone else about this?"

"I haven't found the courage."

Clara spoke slowly, knowing what she said could change her family forever. "The Amish faith is not for everyone. We know this. Our simple and plain ways are meant to keep God first and our families close without the distractions the outside world offers. We are not blind to the world, but we choose to shut it out so that we may live close to God."

Clara cupped Greta's cheek. "You have not been baptized. You would not be breaking a vow if you feel called to seek a different life. Pray about this. It is not a thing to do lightly."

Greta nodded and smiled. "I'm glad you took the

job with Ethan Gingerich. You have much to offer him and his children."

"I pray you are right." Clara realized that she was glad she had accepted the position. It might not be easy, and she might not be there for long, but she would do what she could for the wounded hearts in the Gingerich family.

If Ethan would let her.

Ethan glanced out the window over the sink. Clara hadn't arrived yet. He had been bothered all night by their conversation yesterday. Was she right? Were the children constantly finding trouble because they were bored? Would giving them chores give them a sense of belonging? He could sure use the extra help.

He turned away from the window and looked at the children seated around the kitchen table. "When you lived with your *mamm* and *daed,* did you have chores to do?"

"Sure," Amos said, sitting up straighter. "I fed the rabbits and the goats every day. I hoed the garden, too. *Mamm* always said I did a *goot* job."

"I'm sure you did. All right, I want you all to know that there are going to be a few changes around here, starting today."

"Like what?" Amos asked.

"For one thing, you are all going to have chores to do from now on. Amos, you will take care of the chickens, geese and turkeys. That means you will feed and water them, and you will gather the eggs every day. You will let them out of the pen and make sure they are all back in the roost by evening. Micah, I want you to clean out the horse stalls while I'm gone and make sure there is fresh straw laid down every day. It wouldn't hurt to mow the yard, either. I have a reel mower in the shed."

Micah didn't say anything, so Ethan said, "You will also be responsible for bringing in firewood for the stove. I will cut it. I don't want you swinging an ax until you're older. Amos, you are to weed the garden. Clara can help you if you aren't sure what to do."

"What about me?" Lily asked.

"You are to help Clara with the housework. All of you will need to pick up your rooms and make your beds every day. That includes today if you haven't done it already. And I want you to bring your dirty laundry to the back porch on wash day." He waited for protests, but the children remained silent.

So far so good. Maybe Clara had been right. He wasn't their parent, but he was the adult in charge of them. His horses needed to know who was in charge. They needed clear directions to follow in order to work as a team. Maybe it was the same with children.

He heard the sound of a horse and buggy outside.

He glanced out the window and saw Clara go by in a two-wheeled cart pulled by a palomino pony.

Lily got down from her chair and raced to the door. "Clara's here!"

Amos followed her out the door. Micah remained at the table. Ethan leveled a stern look at the boy. "Today will be a better day for Clara. Is that understood, Micah?"

"I guess." His reply lacked enthusiasm.

"*Goot.* I'll go put her pony away."

"I can do it." Micah got up from the table and went out.

At least Micah wasn't arguing with him. It seemed like a step in the right direction. Ethan was willing to take whatever he could get. He rose and stoked the coals glowing in the stove. He added a small amount of wood so that it would be ready for Clara.

"*Danki,* Ethan."

He hadn't heard her come in. He turned around and was caught off guard by her bright smile. She wore a dark pink dress today and a white apron. It brought out the color in her cheeks and made her eyes an even brighter blue. She carried a large basket over one arm. She came into the room and set the basket on the counter.

It was strange to see a woman enter his kitchen as if she belonged there and yet it was nice. He closed the lid of the firebox and then yanked his stinging fingers away from the hot metal. He stepped to the sink, turned on the cold water and stuck his fingers under the cooling liquid. He glanced at her from the corner of his eye. She hadn't noticed his blunder. She began unpacking her basket.

He said, "I thought I would give you a head start on your day."

"It is appreciated, as is Micah's help with Buttercup."

"I noticed you decided to drive today."

She shot him a sheepish grin. "My grandfather insisted. Normally, I enjoy walking wherever I need to go."

"You mean you don't like driving." He leaned against the counter as he dried his hands. His fingers still smarted. They were red but not blistered.

"I don't. Does it show?"

"Not really. It was a guess on my part."

"A good one. I thought it would be best if I had some means of quick transportation in case anything happened to one of the children."

"My mares are here."

She looked shamefaced and fastened her gaze to the floor. "I know, but I don't think I could bring myself to use one of them. They're so…big."

"You might feel differently if you got to know them. They really are gentle animals."

She gripped a jar of jelly so tightly that her knuckles stood out white. He was afraid it might shatter. He stepped close and took her hands to gently pry the jar from her. A rush of warmth filled him as his fingers closed over hers.

Her gaze flew to his face. Her eyes widened with shock. She opened her mouth, but didn't speak.

He leaned closer, concerned by the look of fear that appeared on her face. "Clara, what is it?"

Chapter Seven

Clara stared into Ethan's face, mesmerized by the emotion in his eyes and his overpowering size as he leaned close. He held her hands. She tried to pull away.

Suddenly, she was back in her uncle's house. Rufus, the horrible man determined to marry her, had followed her into the pantry. He grabbed her and used his weight to press her against the wall, clapping a hand over her mouth to stifle her cries. He began kissing her neck. She cringed and struggled harder. He laughed at her ineffective efforts to escape him.

"Stop it! Let me go!" Clara jerked her hands free. The jar she held crashed to the floor and splintered, splattering blueberry jam everywhere. She crossed her arms tightly and stumbled backward until she hit something solid.

"Clara, what's wrong?"

The image of Rufus faded. Clara realized she wasn't in her uncle's home. She was in Ethan's kitchen, backed into a corner and cowering in front of him. Ethan stared at her in wide-eyed shock.

"I…I need some air." She rushed out the door and grabbed the post on the front porch to keep from falling. Lily and Amos were coming up the steps toward her.

"Micah put your pony in the barn. I like your pony. He's so pretty. I wish I had a pony like that," Lily said.

Don't frighten the children.

Clara drew several quick deep breaths. She let go of the post and sank onto the top step. She drew the little girl onto her lap to hide her shaking hands. "He is a very pretty pony. His name is Buttercup. Someday, your *onkel* Ethan will buy you a pony and cart, too."

"Will you, *Onkel* Ethan?" Lily looked over Clara's shoulder. Clara knew he had come out and was standing behind her. What must he think of her outburst? Nothing like it had ever happened to her before. It had been so real. Was she going insane?

"If you are a good girl and do all your chores I may buy you a pony one day."

"What about me?" Amos asked.

Clara put her arm around him and pulled him close. "You will not want a slow pony and cart.

You'll want a high-stepping, flashy horse and a sporty courting buggy."

"And all of it will cost me a pretty penny," Ethan said. "I had best get busy and cut down some trees to sell. Clara, are you all right?"

"*Ja.* I was dizzy for a moment, that's all. I'm better now."

"Are you sure?"

She wanted to slink under the porch and hide in shame. Instead, she released Lily and Amos and rose to her feet. She took a slow, deep breath, but she still couldn't look at Ethan. "I broke a jar in the kitchen, children. Please wait out here until I get all the glass picked up."

Ethan stepped aside as she walked past him and back into the house. She got a broom and dustpan and began sweeping up the glass and jam, making long smears of purple-blue across the plank floor. She knew Ethan had followed her, but she kept her gaze on her task.

"I'm sorry that I frightened you, Clara. It won't happen again." There was such remorse in his words. It only added to her shame.

She stopped her work and looked at him. "It wasn't you."

He shifted from one foot to the other. His hands were thrust deep in his pockets. "I don't think I believe that."

She couldn't allow him to blame himself. She

propped the broom against the counter and crossed to where he stood by the door. She laid her hand on his arm. "You must believe me. It wasn't you, Ethan."

The touch of Clara's small, warm hand on his bare skin sent his pulse skittering wildly. Her earnest words made him feel better, but he still didn't understand what had happened. For those few seconds, he had seen abject terror in her eyes. He never wanted to see that kind of fear etched on her face again.

She managed a smile, but he could see it wasn't real. She said, "You should get going. It will be hot later today."

"Don't worry about me. I'll be working in the shade."

"That's right." She stepped back and brushed a few stray hairs away from her face. Her hand trembled ever so slightly, but he saw it.

"I'll be at Elam Sutter's again today. Send Micah if you need me."

"I will. Please don't worry. I'm fine now."

He didn't want to go. "If it's something you'd like to talk about, I can listen."

It looked for a second as if she would confide in him, but suddenly she shook her head and moved across the room to begin sweeping again. "A dizzy spell hardly warrants a conversation. Have a pleasant day, Ethan. I'll see you at supper time."

He had been dismissed. There was something that she wasn't telling him, but was it really any of his business? Not if she didn't want it to be. He decided not to press her.

He went outside and saw Micah sitting on the steps with Lily and Amos. He walked past them, then turned back. "Micah, if anything unusual happens, go to Adrian and Faith Lapp. They'll know what to do."

Micah tipped his head. "Unusual like what?"

"I don't know. If there is anything you can't figure out, go get them."

Micah shrugged. "Okay."

Ethan glanced toward the house. It was the best that he could do. He climbed aboard his logging arch and drove toward the highway. For someone who had been so eager to get back to work, all he wanted to do was turn around and find out what was wrong with Clara. If he hadn't frightened her, what had?

Clara didn't relax until Ethan was out of sight. He must think she was *ab im kopp,* crazy in the head. What other explanation was there for someone who shrieked in terror because a man tried to take a jar from her hand?

But it had seemed so real.

It wasn't real. Rufus could not hurt her here. She gave thanks to God for her deliverance and squared her shoulders. She had a job to do. The children needed her. Ethan had hired her to look after them, and that's what she was going to do. No more dwelling in the past.

During the morning, Lily helped Clara wash the kitchen floor again, swishing the mop around with enthusiasm if not precision. Looking out the window, Clara saw Micah pushing a wheelbarrow out of the barn and knew he was cleaning the stalls. Ethan would find his own workload at home cut in half by letting the children help. Amos happily hoed the garden and brought her four big tomatoes when he was done.

"These are lovely, Amos. *Danki.*" She washed them and set them in the kitchen window.

"I will slice them, cover them with cheese and melt them in the oven for our lunch today. How does that sound?"

"Mighty *goot.*"

"Did you gather the eggs already?"

"Micah did it."

So Micah was helping his younger siblings with their chores. Clara would praise him for that when he came in.

"Can we play catch in the front yard?" Amos asked.

"That sounds like fun, but don't leave without

telling me." Clara sent him out to play while she did some baking. After setting two cakes in the oven, she looked out the window again and didn't see any of the children.

They knew they were not to leave without telling her. Had Micah's rebellious nature gotten the better of him again today?

She went to the front door and opened it. Amos and Lily were sitting on either side of the doorway with their backs to the wall looking forlorn. Clara didn't see Micah. "Where is your brother?"

"Behind the barn," Amos said with a scowl. He held a baseball and a glove.

"He doesn't want to play with us," Lily added.

"He called us babies." Amos tossed his ball into the air and caught it.

"It wasn't nice of him to call you that. What is he doing behind the barn?"

"Getting in trouble," Lily said with a sigh.

Amos pressed a finger to his lips. "He'll get mad at us if we tell."

"Perhaps I should go see for myself what he's doing. I want you to go in and wash up. We will have lunch soon."

When both the children went inside, Clara walked toward the barn. What mischief was Micah up to now?

She paused beside the fence at the corner of the

barn because she saw that the barn door was open. Were Ethan's mares inside?

Clara heard the smacking sound coming from the back of the barn. What was Micah doing?

Since the horses weren't in sight, Clara climbed over the fence and hurried to close the barn door. She latched the bottom half, but before she could get the top shut, one of Ethan's mares stuck her head out.

Clara jumped back, her heart beating wildly. The horse reached her long nose toward Clara. She took another stumbling step back. With a snort of indifference or disgust, Clara wasn't sure which, the mare moved away from the door. Pressing one hand to her pounding chest, Clara skirted the door and went around the corner of the barn.

Micah had his back to her. The smacking sounds she had heard were eggs being tossed into the air and smashed with a baseball bat. The back of the red barn was covered with splattered yolks and bits of eggshells. A pile of unbroken eggs lay by Micah's feet. He must've heard her sharp indrawn breath because he spun around to face her, trying to hide the bat behind his back.

She fisted her hands on her hips. "Micah Gingerich, you just wait until your father gets home."

The boy's guilty expression turned to anger. "He's not my father, and he's never going to be."

He picked up one more egg and hit it before throwing the bat down and running toward the creek.

Clara called after him, but he kept going. Her frustration grew. One minute he was doing his chores and being helpful, the next he was doing something like this. She was more certain than ever that he was struggling with pent-up grief. She wanted to help him, but was she doing more harm than good?

Ethan looped a chain around the section of tree he had finished cutting. After checking that it was secure, he climbed onto his rig and spoke softly to his team. He asked them to back up and they responded without hesitation. When he had his logging arch where he wanted it, he said, "Whoa."

The team stopped immediately, but Dutch shifted his weight impatiently, waiting for the command to pull. He knew it was coming. Ethan hopped off and connected the chain to the pull bar. He was as impatient as Dutch to get the day's work over with. His mind was on Clara. How was she faring with the children today?

He remounted and gave the team the command they were waiting for. Both horses leaned into their collars. The two-thousand-pound log glided along the ground, making a shallow furrow as they pulled it between the trees and out to the collection area beside the road. Tomorrow, the *Englisch* trucker

Ethan occasionally worked with would bring the heavy equipment needed to load and transport the logs to the sawmill.

Ethan unhooked the log and jumped back onto his arch. He turned his team and they trotted back to where he was working. They waited patiently while he prepared a second section of the tree for transport.

"They are an impressive pair."

He looked up to see a young woman standing at the edge of the woods. It was Clara's youngest sister. The one who worked for Elam. "*Danki.* They're good fellows."

She held out a small blue-and-white cooler. "Katie Sutter sent me with your lunch. Where would you like it?"

"On that stump." He pointed toward the tree he'd just cut down. She put the lunch pail where he indicated, but she didn't leave.

She walked to the head of his team, speaking softly to alert them to her presence. Dutch lowered his head to sniff at her pockets. She laughed. "How did you know I brought apples just for you and your friend?" Slipping it out of her apron, she held the apple flat in her hand and offered it to Dutch. He eagerly nibbled it up. She took a second piece of fruit and offered it to Fred, who did the same.

She looked around them to Ethan. "Did you train them yourself?"

"I did. You are Clara's sister, *ja?*"

"I'm Betsy. The youngest of the Barkman clan."

"I thought it was you. My thanks for bringing my lunch out here. I hope it didn't put you to any extra trouble."

"No trouble. I came because I wanted you to give a message to Clara. Greta and I are having supper with Elam and Katie tonight. Grandfather is spending the night in town. Carl received word that a friend is in the hospital. He and Lizzie have gone to visit him."

"I'll give her that message."

"Danki."

He secured his chain and came to stand by his horses' heads. This might be his chance to find out more about Clara. "I see you aren't afraid of my big fellows."

"*Nee,* I love horses of all sizes, unlike Clara. I'm honestly surprised that she drove herself to your place this morning."

"Buttercup is not what I would call intimidating."

She laughed. "That's exactly why my grandfather bought him for Clara."

"Was your sister feeling all right when she left home this morning?"

Betsy's smile faded. "As far as I know. Why?"

"She had a dizzy spell. I would have called it a fright. She looked terrified for a moment. I thought she was going to faint."

Betsy eyed him sharply. "I've never known her to do such a thing."

"Maybe it was more of a strain for her to drive the pony than we think."

"Maybe," she said slowly.

It was clear that Clara's sister didn't believe that any more than he did.

Two hours after Clara had fed Amos and Lily lunch, Micah finally came in. His shoes were muddy, but his red eyes and the tearstains on his face concerned her the most.

She said, "I expect you are hungry."

"A little," he mumbled.

"Do you think that you deserve a meal?"

"I guess not."

At least he recognized that his actions deserved consequences. She carried a tomato-and-cheese sandwich on a plate to the table. "Go wash up. We will talk about this when you come back."

"Are you going to tell *Onkel* Ethan what I did?"

"Nee."

"You're not?" He looked so relieved that she felt sorry for him.

"I'm not going to tell your *onkel.* You are going to tell him. Now go wash up."

Looking dejected, he shuffled out of the room. When he returned a few minutes later with clean hands, he sat down at the table and gazed at her with soulful sad eyes. "Please don't make me tell *Onkel* Ethan. He'll be really mad. He'll…he'll beat me."

Clara sighed and took a seat across from him. "You make your transgression worse by maligning your *onkel.* He is not a cruel man. I know because I was raised by my *onkel* after my parents were killed and he was a cruel man."

"He was?"

Clara nodded. "Like you, I was the oldest. I had three younger sisters to look after. My *onkel* beat us at least once a week. I don't mean a spanking. I mean a beating with a wooden rod or sometimes with a belt."

"Truly?" The look in his eyes said he didn't know whether to believe her or not.

"Truly. My sisters and I had bruises that lasted for weeks. Micah, I bathed your brother and your sister a few days ago and there were no bruises on them. If you show me bruises your *onkel* gave you, I won't make you tell him what happened today."

He sat silent for a long time. Finally, he pushed his plate away. "*Onkel* Ethan has never hit me."

Although she suspected that was the case, it was good to know for sure.

"Why did God do it? Why did He take our parents away? What did I do that was so bad?" He dropped his head onto his arms.

Clara laid a comforting hand on his head. "You did nothing bad, Micah. It was not your fault. I wish I had an answer. We can't know God's plan for us, but we know that He loves us and He will always be with us, even in our sorrow. You will see your parents in heaven and live with them there forever. Until then, you must live your life on earth in a way that will please them. Do you understand?"

He sat up and wiped his eyes. "I guess."

"*Goot.* Now eat your sandwich and then you will go to the henhouse and you will clean out all the straw, and then you will put fresh new straw in all the hen's nests."

"Why do I have to do that?"

"So that you will remember, next time you want to break eggs, what will be in store for you."

"I think I'd rather have a spanking. It would be over quicker and it wouldn't make me all itchy. If I do all that, do I still have to tell Onkel Ethan about breaking the eggs?"

"*Ja.* You do."

Ethan could tell something was up the minute he walked into the house that evening. Clara had been on his mind all day. He had hurried through his work in order to get home as quickly as he could. Once, he narrowly missed getting cracked on the head by a falling branch because he wasn't paying attention to what he was doing.

Micah was sitting at the kitchen table looking as if he wanted to bolt out the door. Clara was at the table with him, mending clothes. She laid her sewing aside and said, "Micah has something that he needs to tell you."

This couldn't be good. Ethan straightened his shoulders and stared at the boy. "What is it?"

Micah rose to his feet and stood tall. "Today, I broke twenty-five eggs. I did it on purpose and I'm sorry."

Ethan glanced at Clara. "Is that it?"

"That's it. I made him clean out the chicken house and put fresh straw in all the nests, so he has been punished." Clara nodded at the boy and he took his seat. He watched Ethan with wary eyes.

If Clara had given the boy extra chores then the matter was closed as far as Ethan was concerned. "All right. You will not do something so irresponsible again, right?"

"*Nee, Onkel,* I will not. May I be excused now?"

Ethan nodded. The boy was up and out the door quicker than a scurrying mouse. Ethan hung up his hat. Clara seemed well enough now. She looked calm and at home in his kitchen.

"Was it a hard day?" she asked.

"Hard enough. I wonder if I will ever get to come home without hearing about some mischief that boy has got into."

"Maybe after he is grown."

"Maybe. How was your day? Any more dizzy spells?"

"*Nee,* and I'm sorry if you were worried about me." She finished stitching a torn sleeve on one of

Lily's dresses and bit off the thread. She rose to her feet. "Supper is in the oven."

Ethan considered whether he should tell her about his conversation with her sister and decided it was best to keep their relationship honest. "I spoke with Betsy today."

"Did you?"

"I mentioned your dizzy spell this morning. She says she's never known you to have one before."

"I wish you hadn't said anything about it."

"I'm sorry. I was worried about you."

"As you can see, I'm fine."

She did look fine. More than fine. It was hard to keep his eyes off her. There was something about her that made him want to be closer to her. It made him want to know her better. He realized it was more than simple attraction. It had been years since he felt this way about a woman. He couldn't help wondering how Clara felt about him.

Not that it mattered. He wasn't looking for a relationship. He had the children and a business to take care of. He did not need another complication in his life. If he followed his inclination to know Clara better, he suspected that she would prove to be a big complication.

She was gathering her things and getting ready to leave. He wanted to wish Clara a good evening, but when he opened his mouth, he said, "Why don't you join us for supper?"

She looked up in surprise. "Why?"

"I almost forgot to tell you. Betsy sent a message. She and Greta are having supper with the Sutters, your grandfather will be in town and Lizzie has gone with Carl to visit a friend in the hospital. You've gone to all the work to fix us a meal, the least I can do is ask you to join us. We can discuss with the children what will happen if you get that teaching position. I haven't broached the subject with them. Honestly, I've been afraid of how Lily will react."

"You must not let that little girl wrap you around her finger."

"I would like to see you put up with her crying for a day and a half. It scares me more than a widow-maker falling on my head."

"What exactly is a widow-maker?"

"It's a tree that is leaning against the one you want to cut down. You have no idea when and if it will fall while you are working around it."

"Your work is dangerous, isn't it?"

"Chain saws, falling trees, half-ton horses pulling two-ton logs. Sure, it can be dangerous if a person is not careful."

"And are you a careful man?"

Was she simply curious or was she worried about him? No one had worried about Ethan Gingerich in a long time.

"I say my prayers. I pay attention to the woods,

my equipment and my horses. A man cannot do much more. The rest is up to God. But you haven't answered my question—will you stay for supper?"

Lily entered the room as he was speaking and began jumping up and down. "Eat with us, Clara. Please?"

"All right, I'll stay."

Clara wondered if she was out of her mind as Lily jumped for joy. Sharing the evening meal with Ethan would be different than feeding everyone at breakfast. It was more intimate.

Going home to eat alone wasn't appealing, but it might be better than trying to swallow food with Ethan watching her.

He looked surprised but pleased by her answer. *"Goot."*

Standing and staring at him like a ninny wasn't going to make the evening go better. She took Lily by the hand. "Help me set the table. Ethan, you and the boys go wash up."

Lily happily arranged the plates Clara handed her, giving Clara a much needed moment to regain her composure. By the time everyone had washed up, she was ready and so was the meal.

Ethan sat at the head of the table with the boys on his right-hand side. Micah sat closest to him because he was the oldest.

The chair on Ethan's left-hand side remained empty. That was where his wife would sit when he married someday. Lily occupied the next chair. Clara took a seat beside her and tried to hide her nervous jitters.

When they were all seated, Ethan bowed his head and clasped his hands. Everyone did the same and prayed in silence. When Ethan looked up, he cleared his throat. It was the signal to begin the meal.

Clara loaded Lily's plate with a little of everything and took only a small portion for herself. She was too nervous to eat. The meal progressed in silence for a few minutes until Micah said, "Rosie could have her foal anytime now."

Ethan nodded. "I'm hoping for a filly."

Amos took a bite of bread and said, "That's who I'll use to haul logs when I'm grown up."

"Don't speak with your mouth full," Clara chided. "So you want to be a logger like your *onkel?*"

Amos nodded. "I do. Our papa was a logger, too. I helped him a lot."

"No, you didn't," Micah said. "You were too little."

"I was not. I helped lots." Tears welled up in Amos's eyes.

Clara tried to ease Amos's bruised feelings. "I'm sure both of you boys were a big help to your father. Ethan, is that why you started logging, because your brother worked in the trade?"

"Our father was a logger. It seemed natural for me to keep working with the horses after he was gone."

Clara felt a shiver crawl down her spine. Of all the things she could imagine doing, working with his huge team wasn't one of them. "Did you finish at Elam Sutter's today?"

"I did. Tomorrow, I will be working at Chuck Marshall's place. He's an *Englisch* fellow who wants some of his trees thinned."

"Why would an *Englisch* fellow hire a horse logger? Don't they use big machinery?" Amos asked. Clara wondered the same thing.

Ethan chuckled. "He hired me because my horses and I are environmentally friendly."

Amos frowned. "What does that mean?"

Ethan leaned toward him. "It means the horses make very little impact on the forest. We don't have to build a road to use horses the way you would to get heavy machinery and trucks into the area. We don't have to clear-cut areas to work in. In a few weeks, it will be hard to tell that the horses and I have been there. In a few years, the trees we leave behind will be worth more per board foot because they will be taller and stronger after the forest has been thinned."

Clara was impressed. "I had no idea that there was so much to it."

"Believe it or not, horse logging is becoming

popular with the *Englisch*. Well-trained teams can fetch a fine price, and a trainer can earn a fair living. I hope I can always log with my four-footed friends, but it's smart to diversify. Raising and training Belgian teams will give me a second income, and I won't have to travel so much."

Clara looked at Micah. He was pushing his food around on his plate but not really eating. "Micah, do you plan to be a logger and a horse trainer, too?"

He shrugged. "I don't know. I need a job I can start doing soon."

"I'm sure that your *onkel* would be happy to have you working by his side." She waited for Ethan to agree. When he didn't, she shot him a pointed look and arched her brow. He took the hint.

"*Ja,* I would like that very much when you are a little older," he said quickly. "But the choice will belong to you, Micah, and to you, Amos. There are many fine trades a man can learn. You can be a cabinetmaker or a carpenter. You can work for an *Englisch* business or own your own."

Lily tried to stab a carrot stick with her fork. "I don't want to cut down trees."

Ethan reached ovcr and tugged the ribbon of her *kapp*. "You want to grow up and marry a handsome fellow and raise lots of babies."

"Only if they don't cry," she said. She gave up trying to use her fork and picked the carrot up with her fingers.

"All babies cry," Ethan told her.

Lily turned to Clara. "Do they?"

Clara nodded. "I'm afraid so."

"Is that why you don't have any?"

Clara felt herself blushing at Lily's innocent question. "I don't have any because I'm not married."

"Why aren't you married?" Amos asked.

"That's a personal question, Amos, and none of our business," Ethan said. Clara gave him a grateful look.

Lily held her carrot stick up to examine it. "I might want to raise rabbits, then. They're quiet." She popped the vegetable into her mouth and crunched loudly.

Clara chuckled as she and Ethan exchanged amused glances. She realized her jitters were gone. Was it time to discuss how long she might be with the family? She spoke to Micah. "Are you eager for school to start?"

"Not really."

"Because you won't know many of the children?"

When he nodded, she said, "I feel the same way. I applied for a teaching job at Walnut Creek school earlier this summer. If I get the job, I'll have to learn who everyone is and remember their names."

Micah frowned at her. "How can you be a teacher all day and take care of us?"

"She wouldn't be able to do that," Ethan said.

"Clara only agreed to help us until she finds out about her other position."

Micah focused on his plate. "So you might be leaving us soon?"

Clara couldn't read his expression. Was he upset or glad. "I might be. Then again, I might not get the job."

"I want to go to school," Lily said.

"Me, too," Amos added.

"When you turn six you can go to school all day," Clara assured them.

"Okay." Lily started in on another carrot stick.

Clara shared another amused glance with Ethan. He really did have a nice smile. What did he do for fun?

He should take the children to the Independence Day fair that was coming up in Hope Springs. It would be good for them to do something fun together as a family. She decided not to mention anything in front of the children in case Ethan didn't like the idea, but she tucked it away in her mind to bring up later.

After the meal was over, she began to clear the table, but Ethan stopped her. "You've done enough for one day. We can finish this."

"It won't take long." Clara continued gathering the dishes. She wasn't used to leaving work undone.

"Stop, Clara. You were our guest this evening." His tone was stern, but his expression was kind.

"I don't mind," she assured him, and picked up his plate.

He took it away from her. "I do. Micah can finish clearing the table. I'll do these later." He carried the plate to the counter and began filling the sink with water.

Micah came around the table and started picking up the silverware. Clara leaned close to him and whispered, "I'm sorry. I know it is woman's work."

A reluctant smile tugged at the corner of the boy's mouth but he was able to subdue it. "It's okay. I used to do it for *Mamm* all the time."

"I know she appreciated it as much as I do." Clara gathered her things and tied her dark bonnet over her *kapp.* The day had had some rough moments, but it had ended in a good place. Perhaps things would go better for all of them after this.

Ethan turned off the water when the sink was full. "I'll harness Buttercup for you."

"Danki."

He held the door open for her. As she walked past him, her jitters returned in full force. Could it be because she was beginning to like him? More than a little?

The thought was unnerving, but she realized it was true. She did like him. A lot. He was an attractive man, and kind, too. She wondered why he didn't have a wife.

What did he think of her? She was afraid to contemplate that answer after the way she had acted that morning. At least he thought enough of her to let her continue caring for his children. She needed to remember that she was here for that reason alone and not to foster an infatuation for Ethan.

When he had Buttercup hooked to the cart, he came around to her side and held out his hand to help her in. It was a simple gesture. One that dozens of men had done for her in her lifetime. Only none of them had been like Ethan. None of them made her heart race the way Ethan did as his hand closed around hers.

Chapter Eight

Ethan held Clara's hand slightly longer than he needed to as she climbed aboard her cart. He was reluctant to let go. He studied her face carefully. This time there was no fear in her eyes. Instead, he saw a warm glow that made him wish she wasn't leaving so soon. She slipped her hand away from him and picked up the reins. He tried quickly for a way to prolong the conversation. He patted the cart wheel. "Be careful driving home. The *Englisch* drivers go faster and faster these days."

"I am careful. I keep to the side of the road as much as possible. My cart is narrow, so they can pass me easily."

"How does Buttercup handle in traffic?"

"About like this." The pony was standing with one hip cocked and his head down. His nose almost touched the ground. He could have been asleep on his feet for all the energy he displayed.

Ethan chuckled. "Maybe you should get an extra-large slow-moving-vehicle sign for the back and one that says Please Don't Honk. Pony Sleeping."

"Sometimes I think I would get home more quickly if I put him in the cart and got between the traces myself."

He smiled at that. She had a charming sense of humor. The smile that gently curved her lips intrigued him. Hopefully, he would see it more often in the coming weeks.

She glanced his way. "I didn't want to say anything in front of the children, but a week from this Friday is the Fourth of July. There's going to be a celebration in Hope Springs. I hear that many Amish families in this area plan to attend. Will you be going?"

It was almost an invitation. She was overcoming her shyness around him, and he liked that. "I do intend to take the children. I know they'll enjoy the activities."

"It will be good for all of you."

He leaned on the wheel of her cart. "Is your family going?

"As far as I know. I'm not sure about my grandfather. He is something of a recluse. He doesn't care for crowds."

"Perhaps his new wife will convince him to brave the masses."

"You might be right. Naomi loves market day and chatting with everyone who is there."

Ethan racked his brain for another subject. In the lull, Clara said, "I should get going. I'll see you tomorrow."

He had no choice but to step away from her cart. "Until tomorrow."

He watched her drive away, beset with a sense of loss and a burning desire to see the sun rise again.

Clara was up early the next morning, eager to return to Ethan's house. Eager to see him. She actually felt like singing, but she refrained. Lizzie was still asleep on the other side of the bed. It was hard for Clara to remember the last time she had felt so happy.

After brushing out her nighttime braid, she wound her long hair into a coil at the back of her head and secured it with pins. She settled her prayer *kapp* on her head and pinned it, taking a moment to pray for Ethan and his children as she did so. It was still dark outside the windows, so she slipped from the room without waking her sister. To her surprise, Greta and Betsy were waiting for her at the kitchen table.

She smiled at them. "I've never known you two to be up before me."

Betsy and Greta exchanged a serious look. Clara's mirth drained away. "What is it?"

Greta placed her hands on the table and interlaced her fingers. "Betsy told me that she spoke with Ethan Gingerich yesterday."

"I know. He gave me your message, Betsy." She walked to the cabinet and took down a mug. She already knew what they wanted to speak to her about, but she wasn't eager to visit the subject.

"Ethan told me you had a dizzy spell. He said you looked terrified. What's going on, Clara? Are you sick?"

She kept her back to her sisters as she added a tea bag to her mug and poured hot water from the kettle that was always kept warming on the back of the stove. "He was making a mountain out of a molehill. It was nothing."

"Clearly, it was enough to worry him," Greta said. "Did he frighten you, Clara? You can tell us if he did. You don't have to go back there."

Clara turned around to see her sisters watching her intently with deep concern in their eyes. She sighed. "You are going to think that I'm crazy."

"No, we won't," Betsy assured her.

"I don't know why not, for I think I must be crazy."

"Tell us what happened," Greta said gently.

"One minute I was standing in Ethan's kitchen with a jar of jam in my hand. In the next second, I was back in our *onkel's* house. I was in the pantry getting something off the shelf and Rufus came in. He grabbed me and put his hand over my mouth.

"It wasn't real, but it felt so real. I could smell him. I started shouting and trying to get away from him. When I opened my eyes, I was backed into the corner of Ethan's kitchen. He was looking at me like I was a madwoman. Am I a madwoman?"

She desperately needed to know what had happened to her. Maybe she shouldn't be taking care of the children.

Greta got up from the table, took the mug from Clara's hands and set it on the counter, then she put her arms around Clara and hugged her tight. "You are not insane. It's called a flashback, and it can happen after any traumatic event."

"A flashback." It had a name. Somehow, that made it easier to think about.

Greta held her at arm's length and gazed into Clara's eyes. "Did you get away from Rufus that day?"

Clara knew what her sister was asking. She nodded. "He had no chance to harm me for our *onkel* came in, but I knew his intention."

Greta pulled Clara into another hug. Betsy raced to join them and embraced them both. "I praise God for His mercy."

Clara allowed her sisters' love and compassion to seep into the wounds she carried.

When they drew back, Betsy asked, "Why didn't you tell us this sooner?"

"I was so ashamed of what happened. I thought it was somehow my fault."

Greta shook her. "The shame was not yours. The shame belongs to Rufus. You did nothing wrong."

A huge weight lifted from Clara's heart. She hadn't realized how heavy the burden had been until this moment. Clara gazed at Greta. "Will this flashback happen to me again?"

"It's possible, but now that you have shared what happened to you, the healing can start. You must let us know if it happens again."

"I will." She laid her hands on Greta's and Betsy's cheeks. "The Lord truly blessed me when He gave me little sisters to look after. I had no idea He sent them to look after me, too." Her words triggered another round of hugs.

"I can't believe you are all up already, what's going on?" Lizzie asked from the doorway as she rubbed sleep from her eyes.

Clara held out her arm, inviting Lizzie into the group. "Come and we will tell you all about it."

Surrounded by her loving family, Clara was able to tell the story again without the fear and shame that had kept her silent before, and she thanked God for the blessings of her sisters.

The rest of the week flew by for Clara. The little children adjusted well to her presence, and even Micah seemed to tolerate her. He had only one outburst. It wasn't as bad as his previous behaviors, but she sensed he was still angry inside.

Ethan stayed for breakfast each morning and Clara joined the family to share the meal. They were able to discuss what needed doing around the farm that day and make sure each of the children understood any new tasks that they were being assigned. On Saturday, Clara stayed for supper and this time Ethan allowed her to clean up afterward… with his help.

He dried the last dish and put it in the cupboard. It had taken much longer than usual to finish the chore, but neither of them was in a hurry. He said, "I spoke to your grandfather this afternoon and we walked over the areas he wants thinned out. I plan to start work there on Monday. It's not a big grove, but there is enough timber to keep me busy for two days. Do you want to come here and spend the days with the children or would you rather I bring them with me and you can watch them at your home?"

"It would be fun to have them at my place. It will give them new places to explore."

"And hide," he said. They shared an amused glance.

"How are you going to keep Lily from trying to sneak a lamb home?" she asked.

He chuckled. "I'm depending on you to keep

your grandfather's flock intact. Are you sure you don't mind?"

"Not at all. My sisters will want to help and that will make my job easier."

"*Goot.* I will bring the children to you until I have your grandfather's timber cut and hauled out."

He was quiet for a few moments as she wiped down the counters and table. When she laid her dishcloth over the faucet, she was done. There wasn't any more work for her to draw out. It was time to leave.

He leaned against the counter. "It's been a good week for me, Clara."

She blushed. "For me, too."

"If I had known how much easier my life would be with a nanny I would have hired one weeks ago."

A nanny. Any nanny. Not specifically Clara Barkman.

She couldn't suppress the small twinge of dismay his words caused, but she quickly told herself it didn't matter. She wasn't seeking praise. Another woman could have done the job as well as she. It was prideful to think otherwise. If she was hired as the new teacher, another woman would take her place with this family.

Her sister Betsy had worried that the children might become too attached to her, even in a few short weeks. No one mentioned that Clara might become too attached to the family. She needed to keep her emotions in check. She was the hired girl, nothing more. With that thought in mind, she gathered her things and went to the living room. "Micah, please hitch up my pony."

"Okay." He reluctantly went out.

"Is everything all right, Clara?" Ethan was watching her closely.

"Of course. Why do you ask?" She stood by the door waiting to leave as soon as Micah brought the cart around. She didn't look at Ethan.

"No reason. Have a pleasant Sunday."

"The same to you." *Hurry up, Micah.*

A few minutes later, he came in to tell her Buttercup was waiting outside. Clara said good-night to him and started out the door. She paused to look back. Ethan and Micah had gone to the living room. Ethan took a seat in his wing-backed chair in front of the fireplace and opened the newspaper. Micah sat on the sofa and opened a book. Lily came to Ethan with a book of her own. "*Onkel* Ethan, will you read me a story, please?"

He put his paper aside and lifted the girl onto his lap. Amos came and wiggled into the chair beside them. Micah closed his book and moved closer to them on the sofa.

Clara smiled softly as she closed the door. Ethan was slowly finding his way to becoming a parent and she was glad for him. He would be a good father if he just gave himself a chance. He needed someone to believe in him the way her sisters believed in her.

It was too bad that she couldn't be that person.

Chapter Nine

Early on Sunday morning, Clara piled into the back of her grandfather's buggy along with all her sisters. Her grandfather and Naomi sat in the front. The trip took nearly an hour, for it was at the home of Daniel Hershberger and his wife, Susan, on the other side of Hope Springs. Daniel was a prominent businessman in the community. A few people complained that he wasn't humble enough for an Amish man, and that his successful business made him prideful, but his wife was everything Daniel was not. A plain woman who had married late in life, Susan was modest, humble and able to keep her husband's extravagance in line.

Although it was a little before eight o'clock in the morning when Clara's family arrived, it was already growing warm. Instead of using the Hershbergers' home for the service, the men were finishing arranging the long backless benches in the lower level of Daniel's barn. The large doors were open at both ends of the structure to allow the breeze to blow through. The benches were divided into two sections, one for the women and one for the men. A few chairs had been carried out from the house for some of the elderly members.

Clara and her sisters took their places among the unmarried women and girls near the back in their section. The current schoolteacher, Leah Belier, came in and sat in front of Clara. Beside her was Joy Mast, a young girl with Down syndrome. Joy proceeded to say hello to everyone close to her with waves and hugs.

Leah, like Clara's sister Lizzie, planned to marry in the fall. Leah would wed Joy's father, Caleb Mast. She smiled at him across the aisle and he smiled back. It was easy to see they were in love. His daughter ran to hug him. He gave her a quick kiss on the cheek and sent her back to Leah. Although most Amish engagements were kept secret by the young couples, Joy had announced, to everyone's amusement, her father's intention to marry her teacher at the school Christmas program last winter.

As Clara watched Leah rein in Joy's exuberance, she realized that Leah, with her years of experience as a teacher, might be able to give Clara some insight into dealing with Micah's behavior.

She decided to make a point of speaking to the teacher when the preaching service was over.

Clara glanced at her sister. Lizzie was smiling, too. Not at Joy's antics, but at Carl King sitting across the aisle. Clara sighed. It would be nice if Ethan and his family belonged to the same church district so that she could see them on Sunday as well as every other day of the week. It was her first morning away from them, and she was missing them already.

The whispering and rustling among the congregation grew quiet when Bishop Zook and the two preachers came in. Clara picked up the Ausbund from the bench beside her and opened the hymnal as she waited for the singing to begin. Throughout the three-hour service, she found it hard to keep her mind on the bishop's and the preachers' words as they took turns speaking about God's presence in their lives. More often than not, thoughts of Ethan intruded. He would be attending a service much like this one. Was Lily behaving? Were Amos and Micah fidgeting, eager for the preaching to end? Would they make friends after the service and join other children their age in play?

When the preaching was finished at last, Clara and her sisters helped set out the food while the men rearranged the benches and set up tables for the noon meal beneath the shade of several large trees at the side of the house. When she was done with her work, Clara went looking for Leah and found her supervising a dozen youngsters getting ready to play Duck, Duck, Goose inside the barn.

Clara waited until the game was underway before she spoke. "Leah, have you a few minutes you can spare?"

"Certainly. Have you heard from the school board yet?"

"*Nee,* not a word."

"That's odd. A teacher, especially a new one, needs time to prepare her lesson plans for the year. They should let you know something soon."

"Do you know who else has applied?" Clara wondered if there was someone more qualified than she was.

"I believe three other women. Sally Yoder, a newcomer named Melinda Miller and Samuel Stutzman's niece, Deborah Stutzman. He's on the school board, so I have no idea which one of you they will choose. If they ask me, I'll put in a good word for you. I think you would make a wonderful teacher."

"Danki." It was good to have the support of the current teacher, but would the men on the board give weight to Leah's wishes?

Leah kept an eye on the children at play. "It would be unusual for the board not to give the position to someone from this district, but ultimately they must keep the best interest of the children in mind. Samuel's niece has only recently moved here. Sally grew up in this district, but she has something of a flighty disposition, although she always means well."

"I am a newcomer, too."

Leah smiled. "That may be true, but no one would call you flighty. It takes a firm hand to keep a school full of children in line. Do you have a firm hand?"

"I guess I won't know until I'm put to the test. The children are going to miss you, Leah."

"And I will miss them. It's a wonderful, rewarding career if God chooses that path for you, Clara. I pray He will. I would enjoy having you apprentice with me for the first few months of the school year."

Clara knew an inexperienced teacher learned her job working alongside the current teacher rather than through more education. It made the transition much easier for the students and for the new teacher. Clara suspected that having Leah show her the ropes would make a challenging job much more enjoyable.

"In the meantime, I have taken a position helping Ethan Gingerich take care of his two nephews and his niece while he is working. Do you know him?

"I've seen him, but I haven't actually met him. I did hear about his brother's and his sister-in-law's deaths and how Ethan took their children in. I'm glad he has found someone to look after them. How old are they?"

"Lily is four, Amos is five and Micah is eight."

"So only Micah will be in school this year. How are they doing after such a terrible loss?"

"That's something that I wanted to talk to you about. Lily and Amos are doing as well as can be expected, but Micah isn't. The boy is often angry. He can be sweet, but at the drop of a hat, he becomes moody and belligerent. I'm afraid I'm at my wit's end trying to make a real connection with him."

"I'm sorry to hear that, but it's not surprising."

"How do I handle it?"

"Our teachers' newsletter, *The Bulletin Board,* has some very good suggestions for dealing with a grieving child. I'll let you borrow them."

"That would be great."

"You need to remember that children grieve differently than adults. A child may go from crying one minute to playing the next. Playing can be a defense mechanism."

"Like a boy swinging a baseball bat and hitting eggs?"

Leah frowned slightly. "The oldest one?"

Clara nodded.

"It's also normal for them to act out, to feel depressed, even guilty, or angry at the one who has died, or at someone else entirely."

"Micah seems angry at the whole world."

"How old did you say he was?"

"Eight."

"At that age, he will understand that death is final. The younger children may think it is temporary and that the person will come back. Micah may be acting out because he has difficulty talking about his feelings. He may be worried about his own death or feel that he is to blame for the death of his parents, somehow. He's probably worried about who will take care of him and his siblings if something happens to their *onkel*."

"That makes sense. I think he feels he'll be left alone. He overheard Ethan's two aunts say they would each take one of the younger children, but neither of them wanted to take him."

"The poor child. I'm sure he feels powerless and vulnerable. You need to get him to express his fears and help him understand that in our Amish society, people will step up to take care of him and his siblings, for God commands us to care for orphans and widows. Reassure him that God's plan for us is much larger than we can see, but His love is always with us."

"I've tried to do that."

"Make sure that their *onkel* is part of the conversation. As their parent now, he is responsible for helping them cope. His faith is an example for them to follow."

"That's part of the problem, too. Ethan doesn't feel that he can be a parent. He doesn't believe he can replace his brother."

"Then you need to get him to talk about his grief, too. Without his support, it will be much harder for the children."

"I'm not sure how to broach the matter. I'm simply the hired girl." A hired girl who spent far too much time thinking about her handsome employer.

"You will manage. I know you will. Speaking of the school board, I believe I see Eli coming this way. Maybe you're about to hear if you got the job."

The school board president, Eli Imhoff, was walking purposefully toward them. Clara chewed the bottom corner of her lip. She did still want the job, didn't she?

Of course she did. Ethan and his children were a temporary summer position. She needed something to support herself for years to come. She glanced at the children playing around them. To always be surrounded by children was a dream she wasn't willing to give up.

Eli nodded to the two women. "Good Sunday to you both. Clara, I wanted to let you know the board has decided to interview each of the candidates one more time. Will Tuesday the fifteenth work for you?"

"That is fine for me. What time?" Was a second interview a good thing or a bad thing?

"Seven o'clock at the home of Wayne Mast. Leah, will you be able to be there, too?"

"Of course. It's taking a rather long time for the board to come to a decision."

"Replacing you is a difficult task, Leah. It is not something we wish to rush into. I will see you both then." He turned and walked away.

Leah smiled at Clara. "It sounds like we will have our answer before the end of the month. I hope so, anyway."

Clara managed a smile, but she wasn't as excited as she thought she would be. In a few weeks, her life could take another drastic turn.

Ethan arrived at Clara's grandfather's farm just after sunup with the children crowded around him on the small bench of his logging arch. Clara came as far as the front gate to greet them, but she couldn't bring herself to walk past the huge horses. Ethan noticed her hesitation. "They are as tame as your grandfather's lambs."

"I will take your word for it," she said from the safety of the fenced yard.

Micah jumped down, followed by Amos. Lily held on to Ethan's arm, and he slowly lowered her to the ground. "You behave for Clara today."

"We will," Lily and Amos said together. Micah nodded.

"Can we come watch you chop down trees?" Amos asked.

"If Clara wants to bring you out, that will be fine," Ethan said.

It was her chance to spend more time with him. Clara realize how pathetic it was, but she jumped at it. "We will bring you lunch today and have a picnic up at the lake."

He smiled brightly at her and her heart fluttered wildly inside her chest. "That sounds great. Just make sure you don't come too close until I know you are there. I wouldn't want to drop a tree on one of you."

Lily covered her *kapp* with both hands. "I don't want a tree on my head."

"We'll be careful," Clara assured him as she opened the gate to let the children come in.

He touched the brim of his hat. "Until later, then." He spoke softly to the team, and they took off at a trot.

For Clara, the morning passed slowly. The children went willingly with Greta as she did her chores and took care of the sheep. Clara spent the morning preparing a picnic lunch and baking a cherry cobbler because she knew Ethan would like it.

Finally, the hands of the clock moved to noon. Clara gathered her packed picnic basket and blanket and called to the children. They all came running.

Amos tried to see into her basket. "What's for lunch? Is that cherry cobbler I smell?"

She pushed the lid shut and started across the pasture with the boys trailing behind her "You will find out what I have made when we reach your *onkel*."

Lily stayed by her side. When the boys were out of earshot, she tugged on Clara's apron. "Is there cherry cobbler?"

"*Ja,* but don't tell the boys. It's our secret."

"Okay."

Lily's bright smile made Clara's heart contract with love. As much as she might want to remain unattached to the children, it simply wasn't possible.

It took twenty minutes to reach the lake. The boys ran down to the shoreline and began skipping stones across the still surface of the water as Clara and Lily rested on a flat rock. After a little while, she called them together and they started along the path that skirted the edge of the lake. Micah, who had run ahead of them, suddenly shouted for her. "Clara, look what I found."

She rounded a bend in the path and saw him peering into one end of a fallen log. "You found the letter tree."

"No, I found a fishing rod." He pulled a red fiberglass rod and silver reel from inside the trunk and held it up.

"It belongs to Joann Weaver."

Micah tipped his head. "How do you know?"

"I know because I have heard the story."

"What story?" Lily asked.

"About a year ago, Joann lost her new fishing pole in the lake. Someone else fished it out. His name was Roman. He left the pole leaning against this log with a note for the owner if he returned. Joann comes here to fish often. She found the note along with her fishing pole and she was so happy that she wrote a thank-you letter and left it here. They continued to write to each other and leave the letters here in the tree.

"Now, Joann and Roman worked together at the same place, but they didn't really like each other. It wasn't until they discovered they had been pen pals that things changed for them. They still come here to fish."

"Did they get to be friends?" Amos asked.

Clara smiled. "They got to be much more than friends. They fell in love and they got married. Joann still keeps her pole here so she can go fishing whenever she can get away."

"That's a dumb story," Micah said.

"Why do you think it's a dumb story?" Clara asked him.

"Because it is." He put the fishing pole back.

"I like the story," Lily said.

"I like it, too. We should get going. Your *onkel* is

probably getting hungry." Clara held out her hand to Lily.

Lily gazed at her with a solemn expression. "Are you going to get married?"

"I don't know. If it is God's plan for me, then I will. If He wants me to be a teacher, then I will stay single."

The idea of marriage used to terrify her even more than Ethan's big horses. Only recently had the thought of spending her life with one man stopped frightening her. She knew Ethan was the reason. She wasn't frightened of him. In fact, she thought about him all the time.

"*Onkel* Ethan is never going to get married, and neither am I," Micah said.

"What makes you think your *onkel* won't marry?" she asked with a frown.

"I heard *Mamm* and *Daed* talking about it once." Micah fell into step beside her on the path.

Clara knew she shouldn't encourage the child to gossip, but she wanted to know everything about Ethan. "What did your *mamm* and *daed* say?"

"*Daed* said that Jenny broke Ethan's heart because she wouldn't marry him so he had to move away. *Mamm* said that he would get over his broken heart, but *Daed* said *Onkel* Ethan wasn't the kind of fellow who would get over something like that. He's the kind of fellow who only loves one woman in his life."

"I hope your papa was wrong about that. I hope your *onkel* Ethan finds a woman who will make him happy and who will be a good mother to all of you."

Lily tugged on Clara's hand. "Why don't you marry *Onkel* Ethan? Then you could be our mother."

Micah spun around, his face twisted with fury. "She can't be our mother! We only had one mother, and God took her away from us. She's dead. Papa is dead. They are never coming back."

Lily burst into tears. Horrified, Clara scooped her into her arms. "Oh, Micah, I never meant to imply that someone could replace your mother. I know that isn't possible. I'm sorry if you thought that was what I meant."

"I hate God. I hate Him for taking them away. Why didn't He take us with them so we could all stay together?" Tears were rolling down his cheeks. His small frame was shaking. Amos stood to one side looking confused and scared.

Clara patted Lily's back to soothe her. "I don't know why, Micah. I only know that God loves us and that He has things that He wants us to do in this life. Your parents are waiting to see you again. You must do your best to live a life that will make your mother and father happy."

He pressed both hands to his eyes. "I want to know why!"

She knelt in front of him and laid a hand on his shoulder. To her surprise, he didn't shake it off. "We can't understand God's ways. We can only have faith in His love for us."

"I miss them so much." He flung himself into Clara's arms, nearly knocking her over. She hung on to him and to Lily, wishing she could offer them greater comfort but knowing all she could do was hold them. She glanced at Amos and smiled at him. "Come here. We all need to hug each other."

The boy threw his arms around her neck and hung on, too. Everyone was crying. Clara had tears on her cheeks, too. For them, not for herself.

After a while, Micah pushed away from her. He sniffed and wiped his nose on the back of his hand. "You aren't going to tell anyone I was crying, are you?"

"*Nee,* I wouldn't dream of it." She offered him a napkin from the picnic basket, and he used it to blow his nose. She leaned back to look at Amos and Lily. "Are you feeling better, too?"

They both nodded. She rose to her feet. "Let us dry our eyes and find Ethan. He is surely going to be starved by now."

"I'm hungry," Amos declared.

Micah cuffed him gently on the head. "You're always hungry."

Amos brushed his hair into place and grinned at his brother. "I know."

Happy to see that their tears were done for the moment, Clara picked up the picnic hamper and settled it on her arm. She looked around. "I'm not sure where your *onkel* was going to be working."

"It's this way." Micah took off toward a narrow ravine.

Clara caught up with him. "Are you sure?"

"*Ja.* See the hoofprints. Only *Onkel* Ethan's horses have feet that big."

She glanced down. He was right. The tracks were unmistakable. Walking single file along the creek that tumbled over a rocky streambed, she and the children soon heard the sound of Ethan's chain saw. A few minutes later, they climbed into a small clearing. Ethan didn't see them. He was intent on cutting through the tree. His horses stood off to the side of the path, waiting patiently for their chance to start working.

Clara judged she and the children were far enough away from the trees to be safe. "We will wait here until your *onkel* is finished."

The words were barely out of her mouth before the tree came crashing down. Amos glanced at her with a huge grin on his face. "That was awesome."

Lily looked up at Clara. "If we cut down all the trees, where will the birds sit?"

Clara grinned at her. "Good question."

Ethan spotted them at that moment and waved. She waved back, suddenly eager to spend time with him again. Was he a man who could only love one woman or was his brother wrong? She had no way to answer the question. The only thing she could do was guard her heart against caring for him more than she already did.

He pulled his yellow ear protectors down around his neck. "I was beginning to wonder if you had forgotten me."

She put a smile on her face. "I'm sorry we're late."

"I will forgive you if you brought me some of that cherry cobbler I like so well."

She pulled a long face. "Cherry cobbler, I don't know…"

Lily tugged on her skirt. "Yes, you do. It's in the basket."

Clara pretended to be disappointed. "That was our secret. Now we have to share it with him instead of keeping it all to ourselves."

Lily shook her head. "You know we must share with those less fortunate."

Clara met Ethan's amused gaze and burst out laughing.

Ethan had seen a few tentative smiles from Clara, but he'd never heard her laugh. The sound of it made his grin widen. She needed to laugh more often. Sometimes she was much too serious.

He stepped forward and took the picnic basket from her. "Come, I have a table ready for us."

"You do?" She looked as if she didn't believe him.

He cocked his head toward the tree he had just finished cutting down. "The stump will make a pretty good table. I'll have some chairs cut in a jiffy."

He trimmed one of the logs he had cut earlier into sections and arranged them around the stump. Clara spread her quilt over the makeshift table. "I love the smell of fresh-cut wood."

She opened the hamper and began to set out lunch. There was fried chicken, fresh-baked bread that was still warm, corn on the cob and her cobbler. She reached into the basket and pulled out two fresh apples. "I thought your horses might enjoy a treat, too."

He was surprised by her thoughtfulness. "*Danki.* You may feed it to them yourself if you'd like."

She quickly shook her head.

"I'll feed them," Micah said, and held out his hands.

She handed the apples to him. "Be careful. They are very big animals."

"I'm used to them. You should learn not to be scared of them." He walked to where the team was waiting.

"He's right, you know," Ethan said.

Clara shook her head. "Some things are easier said than done. Overcoming a fear, even a senseless one, is not so easy."

Ethan didn't have a senseless fear to overcome. His was real and soul deep. No matter how much he cared for someone, how much he loved them, he was never loved in return. He needed to remember that when Clara's smile tempted him to think otherwise.

Chapter Ten

Clara noticed a change in Ethan's attitude during the meal. She couldn't quite put her finger on what it was except he seemed cooler, less friendly, but only when he was speaking to her, not when he spoke to the children. He gave them his undivided attention, and she felt a twinge of envy.

What had she done wrong? The mantle of insecurity and trepidation she tried so hard to shed slipped over her shoulders again. As soon as Ethan was done eating, she quickly began to gather the dishes and repack her basket. "We should get going, children. We have kept your *onkel* Ethan from his work long enough."

A pained expression flashed across his face, then was gone. He rose to his feet. "There's no rush. The horses could use a longer break."

She wanted to stay, but she wasn't sure if he meant it or if he was simply being polite. Knowing how much he cared about his horses and his work, she decided to test a safe topic. She gestured to the grove of trees. At least a dozen trees that had been marked with a yellow *X* were still standing. "What is it that you're doing here?"

"It's called restorative forestry. I'm doing single-tree selection. What do you see when you look at this grove?"

"Trees."

That pulled a grin from him and made her happy. "Trees marked with yellow paint," she added quickly.

"Those are the ones I plan to harvest."

She left her basket on the stump and moved to stand beside him. "Some of them don't look as if they would make good lumber."

"That's right." He seemed pleased with her comment. It gave her courage a boost.

"If you aren't taking trees for the best lumber, what are you doing?"

He swept his arm toward the hillside. "This grove hasn't been logged in fifty or sixty years, maybe longer. Because of that, we have what's called an uneven-aged stand. Some very old trees all the way down to saplings sprouting where they can."

"Is that bad?" Clara glanced around to check on the children. Micah and Amos were petting the horses. Lily was sitting on her log chair playing with several cups on the tabletop.

"It's not bad. It's the way a forest develops naturally. Your grandfather wants to maintain that, but gain a little income from the lumber. My job is to take out diseased trees, storm-damaged trees and ones that are overcrowded. That will allow the young trees to grow stronger and faster. In a few years, they'll be worth a lot more. Good trees can be harvested out of here every ten to twenty years this way. He's looking ahead, protecting an investment and a forest at the same time, not just gaining all he can from a clear-cut."

"Why have you marked some of the big ones?"

"I'll also fell some of the most mature trees, like a few of those black walnuts. They're high-quality veneer woods. They'll bring a pretty price at the sawmill. The other trees will be used for firewood, posts and poles or pulpwood."

"Veneer as in furniture wood?"

He nodded and hooked his thumbs through his suspenders. "Authentic handcrafted Amish furniture. I'm pleased to be a part of that."

"I can understand why."

It was pleasant here in the dappled shade cast by the forest. A rich, loamy scent hung in the cool air and mixed with the pungent odor of freshly cut wood. Last year's leaves and fragments of walnut shells made a noisy carpet on the forest floor. A pair of squirrels dashed across it from one tree to the next in search of food or just for fun, scattering leaves as they ran.

Clara could see why Ethan enjoyed working in the woods. It wasn't quiet. Tree branches creaked overhead, birds sang, leaves rustled in the wind, but it was a serene place.

"Those walnuts are massive. Can your horses pull those out after you've cut them down?"

He began walking toward his team. Clara stayed by his side. "I normally cut my logs to under three thousand pounds and about eight and a half feet long. My fellows can pull that weight for about a thousand or fifteen hundred feet without trouble. If the ground is like this, with a little slope in their favor, they can go farther. If I must ask them to go uphill, I cut the logs smaller."

They had reached the boys and the horses. Ethan stopped and rubbed his jaw as he looked at his nephews. "Would you like to watch me cut down a tree? Clara, you and the children go back by the table."

She did as he asked. He picked up a chain saw and walked out to one of the trees he had marked. He slowly circled it, then he looked at her. "Which way should I make it fall to do the least amount of damage to the neighboring trees?"

Clara shook her head. "I don't see any way you can miss other trees completely."

Micah pointed slightly uphill and to the left. "I would drop it in that direction."

"Why?" Ethan asked with a grin for the boy.

"It will miss almost everything except that group of saplings."

"Very good. The saplings are too close together. They won't grow well. They need to be taken out, anyway."

Ethan put his yellow ear protectors on and pulled the chain saw's cord. It roared to life, sending the birds fleeing the area. The serenity of the forest became a thing of the past. He notched the trunk of the tree where he wanted it to fall and then he went around to the other side and began cutting through the wood. He glanced up repeatedly and Clara realized he was watching to make sure the tree didn't topple back on him.

A chill crept down her spine. No matter how much he enjoyed his job, it was dangerous. Particularly for a man working alone.

A sharp crack rent the air as the tall poplar began to fall. Even though Clara was prepared, she was still surprised by the violence of it and the way the ground shook when the tree hit. Ethan stepped up onto the fallen tree and began to trim away the branches. Then he cut the trunk into manageable-sized logs. He killed his chain saw, pulled off his ear protectors and said, "Micah, bring up my team."

Aghast, Clara shouted after the boy. "*Nee,* you are too small to handle them."

Micah just shook his head. "I've been working around horses like these for years."

"Years, my foot." Clara clasped her hands and fell silent. She had shoes older than that boy.

He unfastened their bridles from the trees where they were tied and led the big pair to Ethan. Ethan took the reins, climbed onto his logging arch and, with a few quiet words, he maneuvered the team to back up to the log. Hopping down from his vehicle, he pulled a heavy chain from a box on the back and looped it around the log. He looked at Micah. "Always set the chain so that it rolls the log slightly when the horses tighten it. That way, it takes less work for them to get it moving."

He demonstrated his technique, secured the chain and climbed onto his logging arch. He gave the command and the horses threw themselves into their collars. The big log rolled slightly and then straightened out behind Ethan. It left only a shallow groove in the dirt as he pulled it along. Clara and the children walked down to where he was unhooking the log beside the others he'd cut.

"Very impressive," Clara admitted. He had the horses completely under his control, using only his voice and a light touch on the reins.

"Can I cut down a tree?" Amos asked.

"When you are as tall as Clara I'll consider it," Ethan said.

Amos measured his head against her apron front with his hand. She ruffled his hair. "It won't be long, and you'll tower over me."

He looked pleased with the prospect.

"Can we go home now?" Lily asked. "I'm tired."

They still had a long walk ahead of them. It had seemed like a good idea to have the children wear off some energy on the way to see Ethan, but she hadn't considered that Lily might be too tired to walk home. Clara gathered her basket and hooked it over her arm, then she took Lily's hand.

Ethan said, "It was nice having the children eat with me. We should do this again sometime."

That made her feel better. It wasn't her presence that had upset him. "We will."

"You'll have to bring more of that good cobbler," Ethan said with a smile.

She ducked her head at his compliment. "I'm glad you liked it."

As Clara walked down the hill with the children, Lily began limping. Clara stopped. "What's wrong?"

"My foot hurts."

Clara slipped off Lily's shoe and saw she had a blister on the back of her heel. "I'm sorry, sweetheart. The next time we come I'll drive the cart." Clara realized she was going to have to carry the child. She gave the basket to Micah and lifted Lily.

Amos said, "*Onkel* Ethan is coming this way."

Clara looked back. He was driving toward them. When he pulled up alongside, he said, "Let me give you a lift to the house."

"Yeah!" Amos and Micah climbed onto the tool box behind Ethan.

Clara hesitated. The bench was mighty small. "Lily has a blister on her heel. If you take her, I can walk the rest of the way."

Ethan held out his hand. "No point in that."

"Clara. I want to go home," Lily said with a pout.

It wasn't any different than sharing a buggy seat or a wagon seat, she told herself. Clara nodded and handed Lily up to him. He sat her on his lap and reached for Clara. She put her hand in his and he lifted her easily up beside him.

She was right. The bench was tiny. It was made for one person. She was pressed against Ethan from shoulder to knee. She scooted over as far as she could. He transferred Lily to her lap.

"Ready?" Ethan asked.

The horses started with a jolt. Clara nearly fell off. Ethan threw his arm around her shoulders and pulled her against him. "Careful. I don't want to lose Lily or my best nanny."

Clara could barely breathe. Her heart hammered wildly in her chest, but it wasn't caused by fear. Ethan had his arm around her. Once she had her balance, he moved his arm, but the warm, strong feeling of his embrace remained with Clara for the entire ride home.

Her grandfather came out of the house when Ethan stopped in front of the gate. Clara scrambled down with Lily and moved away from the small cart. Her grandfather eyed her for a long moment before turning his eagle-eyed gaze on Ethan. "How is the logging going?"

"I've got a quarter of the trees felled and cut. I'll be done by tomorrow."

"Goot." Her grandfather patted the hip of the closest horse. "You have a fine team. I hear there will be a horse pull at the Fourth of July fair in town. Are you going to enter?"

"*Nee.* My fellows are working horses."

"They could win, *Onkel* Ethan. I know they could," Amos said.

"Perhaps, but they could also get hurt trying to pull a weighted sled that is too heavy for them. Are you going to the fair, Joe?"

He shook his head. "'Tis a bunch of nonsense and noise. I will stay here where I have peace and quiet."

"Are we going to the fair?" Lily asked.

Ethan nodded. "If you are good for Clara this week, I will take you to the fair."

Lily grinned at Clara. "I'm always *goot.*"

"Me, too," Amos shouted.

"Are you going, Clara?" Lily asked.

"*Ja,* my sisters and I plan to go."

"That's good 'cause it won't be fun without you, will it, *Onkel* Ethan?"

"*Nee,* it won't be fun without Clara," he said quietly.

She hoped he couldn't see how excited she was

by the prospect of spending a carefree day at the fair with him and the children.

On Wednesday, Clara returned to her normal routine. Ethan had finished his work for her grandfather, so she went to his house to look after the children. She arrived early enough to share breakfast with him and the children. After they finished eating, the boys went out to start chores, and Lily went into the living room to play with her doll. Ethan stayed at the table. Clara poured herself a cup of coffee and sat down with him. "What are your plans for today?"

"Adrian Lapp came by last night and asked me to help him clear some deadfall from the creek on his place. We'll cut it up for firewood. There isn't enough to haul to the sawmill. What about you?"

"Cooking, cleaning, counting the children to make sure someone hasn't run off, cooking some more."

He arched one eyebrow. "Are you bored with your job here?"

"Not at all," she assured him. She wasn't. Her work was fulfilling. She took a sip of coffee and realized how nice it was to share this part of the morning with someone who wasn't one of her sisters. She and Ethan were becoming friends, and that was as it should be. She shouldn't look for more.

"Do you think teaching school will be more exciting?" he asked.

"I hope it will be both exciting and rewarding."

"Have you heard from the school board?"

She stared at the cup in her hands. "I have a second interview on Tuesday the fifteenth."

"I hope they hire someone else. Is that bad of me?" He bent sideways and peered out the window.

"You just don't want to break in a new nanny." She turned in her chair to see what he was looking at. Amos was on the barn roof.

Clara shot out of her chair and ran to the door. She heard Ethan laughing behind her. She turned to glare at him. "Do something."

"He got up there. He can get down."

"Ethan Gingerich, you go get him before he falls!"

He unfolded his tall frame from his chair and strolled to her side. He pulled his straw hat from the peg on the wall and settled it on his head before he smiled at her. "Teaching may be more rewarding, but I don't see how it can be more exciting than this crew."

Clara followed him, crushing her apron between her fingers as she willed Amos to stay safely where he was. She was afraid shouting at him might frighten him and make him fall.

Amos sat down with a dejected look on his face when he spotted them. Ethan hooked his thumbs under his suspenders and rocked back on his heels. "What are you doing up there, Amos?"

"Nothing," he answered slowly. He scooted back from the edge.

Clara held up her hands. "Stay still. Don't make any sudden moves. You'll be all right."

Ethan looked around. "How did you get up there?"

"With a ladder."

"Where's the ladder now, Amos?" Ethan asked.

Amos hesitated. Finally, he said, "Micah took it."

"Micah!" Ethan yelled at the top of his voice. Clara jumped.

Micah came out of the barn dragging the ladder behind him. The look on his face said he knew he was in trouble. "I was going to put it back in a minute."

Ethan crossed his arms. "Your minute is up."

"Wow! Can I climb up there?" Lily asked from behind Clara.

Unaware that the child had followed them, Clara snapped at her. "Never! Not ever!"

"Aw! Why do the boys get to have all the fun?" Lily trooped back to the house, dragging her doll by the hand.

Clara glared at Ethan, who pressed a hand to his mouth to cover his grin. "Are you afraid of heights, too, Clara?"

She raised her chin. “A little, and don’t you dare laugh at me.”

“Wouldn’t dream of it.” He picked up the back end of the ladder, then he and Micah set it in place.

Clara’s stomach lurched when she saw Amos stand and take hold of the top rung. Ethan gestured for her to join him. She walked closer. He said, “Come on. Up you go.”

“What?” She took a step back.

“The only way to get over the fear of something is to do it. Climb the ladder and help Amos down.”

“You can’t be serious.”

“He’ll have to stay up there all day if you don’t.”

She took a second step back. “He’s your child. You go get him.”

“You’re his nanny. It’s your job to take care of him.”

She realized they were all grinning at her. She dropped her wadded apron, smoothed the front of it and squared her shoulders. “Nannies do not climb ladders.”

Turning on her heels, she marched toward the house. When she glanced back, Amos was already halfway down. He hadn’t needed any help at all. Ethan and Micah were grinning from ear to ear and slapping their hands together. Laughing, at her expense.

She stomped into the kitchen. “Odious boys.”

Lily was at the table feeding a leftover biscuit

to her doll. "They aren't being good. They should stay home from the fair."

Clara smiled at her and looked out the window over the sink. Ethan had the front of the ladder while Micah and Amos brought up the rear from the tallest to the smallest. Together, they carried it into the barn.

"I should make them stay home, but something tells me I'll enjoy the fair even more if they are there."

The morning of the Fourth dawned clear and bright, without a cloud in the sky. Clara and her sisters giggled and chatted like schoolgirls as they got ready to go to town. They were as excited about spending a day at the fair as any *kinder.* None of them had experienced a Fourth of July celebration. The uncle who raised them believed it was too worldly and sinful. The sisters had only listened to stories told by their friends about the wonders of carnival rides and of fireworks.

As they drove their grandfather's buggy into Hope Springs, the traffic grew heavier and slower as the Englisch cars and trucks were forced to an Amish crawl. No faster than the slowest horse in the line. Greta, the one who was driving, turned off Main Street onto Lake Street. The regular weekly farmer's market was held in a large grassy area next to the town's lumberyard. Today, the area had been given over to the fair. A Ferris wheel towered over the numerous games and booths lined up across the lawn. Tents had their red, white and blue striped sides rolled up to allow the breezes to blow through and fairgoers to view the wares within.

Already a number of tourists were strolling about looking to buy homemade Amish baked goods, cheese, soaps, dried flower arrangements and the ever-popular hand-stitched quilts. Many of the tourists carried cameras, but for the most part, they respected the Amish desire not to be photographed.

Clara kept a sharp lookout for Ethan and the children but she didn't see them. Had he changed his mind about coming?

"I wish Grandfather would have come." Greta steered their buggy into an empty spot.

"Maybe next year," Lizzie said. "I can't believe he talked Naomi into staying home with him. We should do something nice for her. Her birthday is coming up. Why don't we host a party for her?"

"A picnic," Clara said and they all agreed.

"This fair is fantastic!" Betsy's eyes were as big as saucers as she took in the sights.

"What shall we see first?" Lizzie asked.

"Everything," Betsy and Greta said together. They looked at each other and burst out laughing.

If Clara could have used one word to describe the morning, it would've been *frantic*. Betsy and Greta were serious when they said they wanted to see everything. The sisters visited every tent at least twice and even marveled at the shiny farming machinery lined up for display by a local implement company. The sisters sampled candy, cookies and cheese-covered pretzels as well as fresh lemonade.

The sight of a black alpaca tethered beside a tent being put up alerted Clara to where her friend Faith Lapp had her yarns on display.

Clara stopped to talk to Faith's son Kyle and stroke the alpaca's soft fleece while her sisters examined the yarns Faith had for sale. A man's voice said, "I understand they spit."

She knew it was Ethan before she turned around. At the sight of him, her heart gave a funny little jump before speeding up. The whole day grew brighter.

"They only do it when they are upset or frightened," Kyle explained.

Clara stepped between Ethan and the animal and held her hands palms down. "Stay still. Don't make any sudden moves. You'll be all right."

He chuckled. "Are you protecting me from the wild beast?"

"That's what friends do. They do not try to make their friend climb a scary ladder."

"Will I be forgiven for that anytime soon?"

"Maybe, but first I have to know if it was your idea for Amos to climb onto the roof in the first place."

"*Nee,* the *kinder* thought that up all on their own."

"Then you are forgiven. Where are the children?" she asked, looking around.

He gestured toward a nearby tent where ice-cream cones were being sold. Micah, Amos and Lily were waiting in line with a dozen other children. Amos was in animated conversation with another boy his own age. "Amos has made a new friend. His name is Andy Stutzman. I think Lily is feeling a little left out."

"Perhaps she will make a new friend, too."

"Are you enjoying yourself?" Ethan asked.

"Immensely." And much more now that he was here.

"Where is your family?"

Clara looked around for her sisters but they were nowhere in sight. "I don't know. They were here a minute ago."

"So my children aren't the only people you have trouble keeping track of?"

She laughed softly. "Apparently not."

"May I buy my friend an ice-cream cone to make up for teasing her?"

She tipped her head to the side. "I believe you may."

Ethan had many acquaintances in the Hope Springs area but none that he would call a friend. Clara was changing that and so much more in his life.

They could be friends. Their relationship did not have to become complicated. If he was careful, it wouldn't.

They stood in line with the children. It took a while for Clara to make up her mind between strawberry and vanilla, but she eventually settled on strawberry and they were able to go in search of her sisters. The Barkman girls were together at one of the tents. A salesman had convinced Betsy to try his battery-operated steaming floor mop. She looked up, wide-eyed, when she caught sight of Clara. "You have to try this."

"That looks interesting." Clara handed her cone to Ethan and went to join the demonstration. Before long, all four of the sisters were racing to mop a ten-foot-by-ten-foot square of linoleum, and Clara's melting ice cream was dripping over his fingers. It was a small price to pay to see her giggling and happy with her family.

When she returned to him, he handed her the soggy cone. She took it. "I'm sorry I've made a mess for you. Put your hand on the floor, and I'll mop over it."

He pulled a handkerchief from his pocket and dried his hand. "The old-fashioned way works just as well for me. Are you going to buy one?" He tipped his head toward the display.

She grinned and shook her head. "*Nee,* the old-fashioned way works fine for me, too." She turned to the children standing behind him. "On second thought, I wonder if they have one for faces."

Micah was pretty clean, but Amos and Lily had managed to get as much ice cream on their chins and cheeks as they had in their mouths. Ethan put his handkerchief to good use.

The afternoon and evening passed all too quickly. Clara's sisters joined them as they visited the small midway and allowed the children, and the young women, to ride the carousel several times. Clara adamantly refused to step onto the Ferris wheel, but Micah was brave enough to join Ethan on the ride.

As darkness fell, they laid out their quilts on the hillside. Carl King joined them and sat with Lizzie. A young man Ethan didn't know came over to their group. Betsy introduced him as Alvin Stutzman. He settled awkwardly onto the blanket after greeting everyone, but he kept his eyes on Betsy's face.

Clara leaned close to Ethan and whispered, "I think he is sweet on Betsy."

Ethan couldn't decide if Betsy liked the boy or not. "How does she feel about him?"

"I think it is too early to tell."

"I hope she treats him with kindness." He couldn't help the stab of bitterness in his tone.

"I hope he treats her kindly, as well," Clara said, and shivered slightly.

"Are you cold?" He laid his hand over hers.

"I'm fine. It must be the excitement. I've never seen a fireworks display before," she said quickly.

He wasn't fooled. That same flash of fear had passed across her face, but this time she didn't shriek and pull away. "You can tell me if something is wrong."

She quickly regained her composure and squeezed his hand. "I appreciate your concern, my friend, but I'm fine."

The first rocket burst into a shower of sparks overhead. Clara was soon clapping and shrieking with delight just as the children were. He was left to wonder exactly what had caused such fear in her eyes. Would she ever tell him?

Chapter Eleven

The week after the Fourth of July celebration proved to Clara that Ethan and the children were on the right path at last. Micah, although occasionally moody, hadn't caused any trouble and was proving to be helpful. He took good care of Olga and her new calf. He did his chores without being reminded and helped Clara with anything she needed doing around the farm.

With a steady stream of work locally, Ethan was able to be home each evening. Clara stayed for supper twice, but she knew they needed time alone together as a family. Breakfast was her favorite time of the day. It was then that she spent a few cherished minutes alone with Ethan. Their friendship grew steadily, and they became more at ease with each other. Clara knew she would miss their time together if the school board hired her.

More and more, she wondered if caring for

Ethan's children was the path God wanted her to take instead of becoming a teacher. All she could do was pray to follow His will. When the evening of her interview arrived, she chose to walk to the Mast home, hoping the exercise would calm her jitters. It didn't help.

Wayne Mast was waiting outside the door. As the tax collector, it was Wayne's job to ensure the school had adequate operating funds. Her salary, if she got the job, would be paid by him at the monthly school board meetings. Rhonda Mast, Wayne's wife, was in the kitchen slicing a gingerbread cake at the counter. Rhonda was Leah's sister. Wayne was the brother of Caleb Mast, the man Leah planned to marry. The other members of the school board were seated around the table with Bishop Zook at the head. Although not a formal member of the school board, Bishop Zook took an active part in school affairs.

Samuel Stutzman, the treasurer, nodded to acknowledge her. Clara didn't know him well, but she did know that his niece had also applied for the position. Eli Imhoff, the school board president, stood up and came to greet her. Clara was happy to see another friendly, familiar face in the room when she spotted Adrian Lapp. Adrian was the school board secretary. He was seated in a chair beside Leah.

Eli came forward. "Good evening, Clara. Thank you for coming so promptly. I believe this meeting will be brief. We have asked the other applicants to wait upstairs while we conduct the interviews. Rhonda will show you where."

Rhonda pulled a container of whipped cream from the refrigerator and began topping the slices of cake. She arranged them on a tray with some glasses of tea and asked, "Come this way, Clara. I thought you ladies might enjoy a bite to eat."

Clara followed Rhonda to a spare bedroom on the second floor. The windows were open to the evening breeze and the sheer white curtains fluttered softly. Two women sat on the edge of a bed covered with a bright blue-and-white quilt while a third woman sat in a straight-backed chair facing them. An empty chair remained against the wall.

Clara pulled the chair to the group and greeted them. Sally Yoder took the tray from Rhonda and put it on the bed. When Rhonda left, Sally said, "Clara, I believe you know Deborah Stutzman. This is Melinda Miller."

Clara picked up her glass of tea. "Melinda, we haven't met. You're new in Hope Springs, aren't you?"

The tiny woman with white-blond hair nodded. "I moved here when my mother became ill. She's gone now so I'm looking for a position. What about you?"

"I'm so sorry for your loss. I'm the oldest of four

girls, and I have long wanted to take up teaching. I believe it is a wonderful calling."

"It is," Melinda agreed. "What about you, Sally?"

"I've been working as a basket weaver for ages, so I wanted to try something different since none of the men in this area are marriage material."

Deborah laughed. "You mean since Ben Lapp isn't interested in marrying you. You've been throwing yourself at that boy for two years."

"I have not, and if he's not smart enough to catch me, I don't want him anyway."

An uncomfortable silence followed and all of them focused on the cake and tea. Finally, Clara looked at Deborah. "What about you, Deborah? Why do you want to teach?"

"My *onkel* thought I would like the job. My family could use the income."

Rhonda opened the door and looked in. "Deborah, the board would like to speak to you first."

After the two women left, Melinda spoke. "What will you do if you don't get this job, Clara?"

Clara smiled softly. "I'm working as a nanny for a local family. I would like to continue doing that if the Lord wills it."

"I was thinking of being a nanny," Sally said. "I hear some of the *Englisch* families pay very well. Do they?"

"I work for an Amish family so I wouldn't know." Clara was finding it hard to imagine her life without Ethan and his three special children in it. Was teaching the right job for her? Should she withdraw her name for consideration? No, she would wait for God to tell her what to do.

The small talk continued as they waited. Deborah returned after ten minutes. "Clara, they will see you now."

"*Goot.* I hope they make a decision tonight." She put her plate and glass back on the tray.

Deborah shook her head. "They told me I would receive a letter in a few days telling me if I've been hired or not."

A moan went around the room. Melinda sighed. "It seems the good Lord is trying to teach us patience."

A few evenings after Clara's interview, Ethan stabled his horses and faced the house with dread. He spied the clean laundry hanging on the line and breathed a prayer of thanks. He did not want to go into the house looking like this.

He yanked a towel off the line and tossed it over his shoulder to hide his torn shirt and bloody arm. He didn't want to upset Clara or the children. He would clean up once Clara was gone. At least the accident had happened at the end of the day after he'd gotten most of his work done. He wouldn't accomplish much over the rest of the week.

It was a sizable gash, but he had had worse.

Avoiding jagged chunks of wood and falling branches was part of his job. Today, he hadn't done so well. This would put him back a few days.

He drew a deep breath and pushed open the kitchen door. Clara was seated at the table with her hands folded in front of her. He nodded to her. "Evening, Clara, sorry I'm late. You had better get going or it will be dark by the time you get home. I'm going to take a bath."

She stood and folded her arms across her chest. "We need to talk."

"Can't it wait until tomorrow? I'm beat. Go ahead and go home. We can have this conversation in the morning."

"This is not a conversation that can be avoided."

Ethan sighed. "What did Micah do now?"

"He got into a fight with Amos and pushed him down. We need to talk about this."

"Boys will be boys. It's nothing." He could feel the blood dripping down his arm. In a minute, he wouldn't be able to hide it anymore.

"Ethan, you have to talk to Micah about what's bothering him. I told him to wait in his room until you got home. The other children are playing outside. What's wrong with your arm? Why do you have it covered up?"

"Talking to Micah about how he feels won't change how he feels." He walked past her, but she reached out and caught him by the arm. He couldn't hold back a hiss of pain.

She looked down and recoiled in shock as she pulled her hand away. There was blood on her fingers. "Ethan, you're hurt."

"It's nothing. I just need to go wash up."

"Let me see."

"I can manage by myself. Go home, Clara."

"I said, let me see. I'm not going anywhere until I know how badly you are hurt. You're dripping blood on the floor, and I just washed it."

He rolled his eyes. "Have it your way."

He walked to the kitchen sink and unwrapped his arm. The jagged gash ran down the back of his upper arm to his elbow. He tried looking over his shoulder. "I think there may still be a piece of wood in me."

Clara's eyes widened, but she quickly sprang into action. She grabbed a clean towel from the drawer, turned on the water to soak it and began to wash away the blood. "I know this hurts, but we have to get it clean. Roll up your sleeve so I can see what needs to be done."

Ethan did and braced himself as Clara sponged his wound. It didn't just hurt. It burned like fire. "Can you get the splinter out? I couldn't get a grip on it. It's in an awkward place"

"I think I can." She grasped the bloody piece of

wood and pulled. Thankfully, it came out on the first try. "Got it."

He sagged in relief. *"Danki."*

The sound of a strangled cry caused them both to look toward the stairs. Micah stood on the bottom step, his face white as a sheet."

"It's all right, Micah. Your *onkel* has had a small accident." She pressed gently around the edge of the wound. "This might need stitches."

"Are you a good seamstress?" Ethan asked, watching her face for her reaction.

"Me?" she squeaked. "I'm not going to sew you up."

"I'm kidding. It doesn't need stitches. Slap a piece of tape on it and I'll be as good as new in a week."

She pressed a towel tightly against his arm. "Keep pressure on that until I can get something to make a bandage."

"There's a roll of gauze in the bathroom cabinet and some antiseptic stuff."

She left the room. Micah sat down on the step, his face still pale. "What happened?"

"I was felling a tree that was hooked on a widow-maker. A big branch snapped off and came straight down. The jagged end speared me."

Clara came back into the room with the gauze roll and a bottle of iodine. He winced and gritted his teeth when she poured it over the wound. "I'm sorry. I know that hurt."

"I'm fine." He wasn't, but he had to tough it out in front of her and Micah.

Clara made a thick pad with a towel and secured it in place with the roll of gauze as she wrapped it around his arm. He sucked in a quick breath as pain lanced through his wound again.

Clara stopped and looked up at him. He read the worry in her beautiful eyes and something more. A deeper emotion. He lifted a hand to touch her cheek. She didn't flinch or shy away. "I'm okay," he assured her softly.

Clara bit her lip and looked down to continue wrapping Ethan's arm. She didn't want him to see how his touch unnerved her. Or how much she was starting to care about him. He needed a friend to help him, not a weak-kneed woman to swoon over him.

"A widow-maker could kill you," Micah said.

"It's just an expression." Ethan adjusted the pad Clara was trying to secure.

Clara glanced at the boy and saw fear clouding his eyes. It wasn't just an expression to him. "Your *onkel* is fine, Micah. Go check on the children for me, please. They're playing on the swing set out back. Why don't you take them to the cornfield and gather a few roasting ears. I'll make corn on the cob for supper. How's that?"

"Okay."

Micah left and Clara concentrated on Ethan. His corded muscles were rock hard beneath her hands as she worked, yet his skin was soft and warm. She grew warm in turn. She had never touched a man like this. Forcing her mind away from the intimacy of the situation to the urgency, she knotted the bandage in place and went to wash her hands.

He examined her handiwork. "This is as good as any *Englisch* doctor can do."

She quickly dried her hands. "Ethan Gingerich, you will see a doctor if that gets infected, and I don't want to hear another word about it."

His eyebrows shot up. "Are you telling me what to do?"

For a second her courage wavered, but she knew she was right. "If you are too stubborn or too foolish to look after yourself, then someone needs to tell you what to do. There may be more bits of wood in there that will fester. If you were one of my grandfather's lambs with such an injury, he would be the first one to send for the vet. A man deserves as much consideration as an animal. Sit down before you fall down. You look done in."

She waited a second for further protests from him, but none materialized. She went to his bedroom and found a clean shirt. He'd managed to put it on, but she had to button it for him. It was such a wifely thing to do. Her hands began to shake.

Ethan captured Clara's trembling hands with his good one and held them pressed to his chest. "I'm sorry I upset you."

"Accidents happen." She pulled away, carried his torn shirt to the sink and put it in to soak. "I'm not sure I can mend this."

"I have others."

"I received word from the school board." Clara stood with her back to Ethan as she finished filling the sink.

"And?" he asked, although he figured he already knew the answer from the way she wouldn't look at him.

She picked up the dish towel and turned around as she dried her hands. "I got the job."

He wanted to be happy for her, but he wasn't. "I know it is what you wanted. Congratulations. Have you told the children?"

"Actually, I was waiting until you came home. I thought we could tell them together."

"They were just getting used to you."

She sighed deeply. "You knew when you hired me that it might not be a long-term position."

He turned away. "*Ja,* I knew it." Could he help it if he had hoped it would turn into something more?

"I can help you find someone else."

"No matter who it is, it won't be the same. For the children, I mean." It wouldn't be the same for him, either. He had grown accustomed to her in the few short weeks they had been together. Would he feel as comfortable having another woman in his house? It wasn't likely. He glanced her way. He would miss her deeply. In spite of his determination to remain friends, he could feel the pull she had on his heart.

Clara folded the dish towel into a small square. "It won't be the same for the children, but they will get used to someone new the way they got used to me."

Could he talk her out of taking the teaching job? How? He couldn't afford to pay her more. He didn't see any reason for her to stay. He was wishing on the wind. The Lord had chosen a path for her. Ethan would have to respect that. He dreaded telling the children. Lily was going to be crushed. "We should get it over with."

"Why don't we wait? You should go sit down."

"I'm fine. Is there any coffee?"

"Of course."

Ethan took his place at the table. She set the cup in front of him and sat down with one of her own. He would miss this, too, talking to her about the children and about the everyday ins and outs of their lives. It was impossible to imagine finding someone who fit so well with his family. Someone who made him feel…that she belonged with them.

He took a sip of coffee. “Any idea who I should get to replace you?”

“I will ask around at our church meeting on Sunday. Perhaps you could do the same.”

“I reckon that would be best.”

“You could place an ad in the newspaper,” she offered.

“If you and I come up empty, I may have to do that. How much time can you give me?”

“Another week, two weeks at the most. Greta might be able to fill in for a few days after that.”

He nodded and took another sip of coffee. His arm ached, but it was nothing compared to the thought of losing her company, her companionship, her smiling face. She held her mug between her hands and stared at it. It gave him a chance to study her face and memorize the curve of her cheeks, the way her full eyelashes lay like dark crescents on her cheeks when her eyes were closed.

She was someone very special and very dear.

The outside door opened and the children trooped in, their arms loaded with ears of corn. Micah was in the lead. He stopped short when he met Ethan’s gaze. Amos and Lily crowded in around him and brought Clara their prizes.

“I found the biggest ears,” Amos said proudly as he laid them on the table.

Smiling at him, Clara said, "You did a fine job picking them."

Lily added several smaller ones to his pile. "I couldn't reach the big ones."

Clara straightened Lily's *kapp.* "I reckon you found the sweetest ones down low."

Lily grinned broadly. Clara could always do that. She could make each child feel special, and she did it without seeming to try.

Micah stood by the door without moving. His eyes narrowed as he stared at Ethan. Finally, he spoke. "What's wrong?"

"Come sit down, Micah. All of you take a seat. Clara and I have something that we need to tell you."

"What is it?" Amos took a seat.

"Are you going to die?" Lily asked. "Micah said you might die." She stared at her brother standing by the door.

"Nee," Ethan said quickly. "I was hurt by a falling branch, but I'm not likely to die from it."

"That's a relief." Lily climbed into the chair beside Clara.

Micah hadn't moved. Ethan said, "Come sit down."

"I'd rather stand." The boy put his ears of corn on the counter and faced them with his arms crossed.

Ethan shared a glance with Clara. She shook her head slightly so he let the issue slide. He addressed the two smallest children. "Do you remember when I told you that Clara might only work here for a little while?"

Lily shook her head.

"I think so," Amos said slowly.

Micah didn't say anything so Ethan continued. "As it turns out, Clara has to go to a new job soon. She's going to be a teacher."

"That's just great," Micah snapped. "Make them like you and then go away. I'm glad I never liked you." He ran out the door.

Lily and Amos looked confused. Lily stared at Clara. "Why does Micah say you're going away? You're coming back, right?"

Giving the news to Ethan and the children was much harder than Clara expected. "I will be coming back for a few more days, but once school starts, I have to be there every day to teach the children."

Lily looked at Amos and then back at Clara. "But we're children."

"We can still visit each other. Your *onkel* can bring you to visit me at my grandfather's farm, and I can come here to see you on some of the off Sundays. We will continue to be friends, won't we, Ethan?" Clara looked to him for confirmation.

He nodded as he met her gaze. "We'll always be friends."

Amos wore a puzzled frown. "Who is going to take care of us when *Onkel* Ethan goes to cut trees?"

"He is going to find another nice woman to cook and clean and look after you."

Amos got out of his chair. "I don't want some-one else."

"Will she read me a story?" Lily asked.

"I'm sure she will read you lots of stories. Your *onkel* Ethan can read you stories, too."

Lily shook her head as she got down from the table and took her brother's hand. "He doesn't read them as good as you do."

The pair left the room. Clara sighed deeply and looked at Ethan. "That didn't go so badly."

"Except for Micah."

"Except for Micah," she agreed. The boy's words hurt.

"He didn't mean it, you know," Ethan said gently.

"Didn't he?"

"If he didn't like you, he'd be glad to see you go. He likes you, but he's afraid to show it. He likes you much more than he can admit," Ethan said softly. He rose and went to his bedroom.

There was something odd in his voice. Some-thing that made her wonder if he was talking about Micah or himself. She pressed her clenched fist to her chest as the ache of loss overwhelmed her. God had chosen a different path for her, but she didn't know why.

* * *

Finding someone to take Clara's place as a nanny turned out to be easier than Ethan expected. Word got out quickly. Three days later, he studied the young woman sitting across from him at his kitchen table. Her name was Deborah Stutzman. She had applied for the teacher's position, too, but was passed over. Apparently, Clara had suggested she come and see him.

Time was growing short. He needed to find someone to care for the children before Clara started teaching. Someone who understood the children as well as Clara did, but someone who didn't make his heart trip over itself when she walked into a room.

He cleared his throat. "Have you any experience with children?"

"I have six younger brothers and sisters who I help care for."

"I would say that qualifies as experience." He made a note on the paper he held. She wasn't as pretty as Clara. That was a good thing.

"If I would have to be gone overnight for a job, would you be able to stay here?" he asked.

"Oh, *nee,* I could not spend the night."

"Would your parents object if the children had to go home with you?"

She frowned and tipped her head to the side. "I'm not sure. I'd have to ask. Betsy Barkman mentioned that the children had stayed with them before. Perhaps they could stay there again if you need to be gone overnight."

"Are you friends with the Barkman girls?" he asked, wondering how well she knew Clara.

"Betsy and I are becoming friends. My brother Alvin has taken her home after the last few singings. I think he's getting serious."

"I hope for his sake that she returns his feelings." He realized that he wasn't as bitter as he once was about his broken engagement. Was time healing his wounded heart? Or was Clara the cause?

"Betsy likes him, but she says she's going to take her time choosing a husband. She doesn't want to make a mistake the way Clara did."

His gaze jumped to Deborah's face. "Clara was married?"

"*Nee.* The family came here before the wedding took place. Betsy won't talk about the details. She'll only say that she's glad Clara threw him over."

Ethan stood and walked to the window. Clara was out on the porch reading to the children.

She had been engaged and had broken it off.

Some poor fellow was heartsick because of her. The same way he had been heartsick over Jenny.

His feelings for Clara had grown steadily since they met. He told her he wanted her friendship, but as soon as he had that, he wanted more. What a fool he was to let his heart lead him. Hadn't he learned anything? He couldn't believe how close he'd come to making the same mistake all over again. Daring to believe a woman might love him. She was no different than Jenny or his mother. Did she even care about the hurt she caused?

He turned to look at Deborah. "The job is yours. When can you start?"

Chapter Twelve

Clara heard the door open and watched as Deborah came out. She waved but didn't stop to visit. As Deborah drove away in her buggy, Clara put down her book and spoke to the children, "I'll be back in a minute."

Inside, she saw Ethan pouring himself a cup of coffee. "So Deborah didn't work out?" she asked.

He didn't turn around. "I hired her. She starts tomorrow."

"Oh. Why didn't you have her come meet the children?" Clara had hoped to have another week with the family. Another week with Ethan. She wasn't ready for it to be over.

He turned slowly and stayed where he was, leaning one hip against the counter. He took a sip of his coffee. His face had a cold look that worried her. A feeling of foreboding slipped across her nerve endings. "I thought it was best that she meet them without you present."

"Why? Have I done something wrong, Ethan?"

"You never told me that you were engaged and you broke it off. What was his name?"

Clara suppressed a shudder. "I'd rather not talk about it. I don't see why it's important."

"I think it speaks to your character. To pledge to marry a man and then break that pledge shows a lack of integrity. A woman caring for children should be above reproach."

She was being judged for something he knew nothing about. An unexpected rush of anger filled her. "I think this conversation speaks more to your character."

"How so?"

"You have known me long enough to judge my character for yourself. My broken engagement has nothing to do with you, nothing to do with the *kinder.* It's in the past, where I want it to stay."

He turned and poured his coffee down the sink. "You should say goodbye to the children."

Clara started to open the door, but she stopped and looked back at Ethan. Her anger drained away. "I do not want our friendship to end this way. If you see what I did as wrong, then I beg your forgiveness, but I know in my heart that I made the right decision."

She waited for him to speak. When he didn't, she went outside. The children were eager for her to read another story. Tears welled up in her eyes.

She prayed that God would give her the right words for this goodbye.

She took her seat in the wooden rocker, but she didn't open the book. "I have some news for you. Starting tomorrow, you are going to have a new nanny spending the days with you. Her name is Deborah, and she is a very nice girl."

"You'll be here tomorrow, too, won't you?" Amos asked.

She shook her head. "I won't see you tomorrow. We will see each other again, for we are friends, but not tomorrow. Now, I want you to think about ways that you can make Deborah feel welcome in your home. Lily, what special nice thing can you do for Deborah tomorrow?"

"Pick up my toys?"

"That's a nice thing to do for her. Amos, what can you do to make Deborah feel welcome?"

"I can sweep the porch and steps without being asked."

"Excellent." She looked at Micah, who was sitting on the railing at the far end of the porch, not really a part of the group but not too far away. "What about you, Micah? What can you do that will be special for your new nanny?"

He jumped off the railing and landed on the grass. Thrusting his hands in his pockets, he said, "I'll think of something."

He walked away with his head down and his feet

scuffing through the dirt. She didn't know whom to feel sorrier for, unsuspecting Deborah or one hurting little boy.

After kissing Amos and Lily goodbye, she hitched up her pony. She hoped Ethan would at least come out to see her off, but he didn't. She drove away knowing she wouldn't be coming back. Once she was out of sight of the house, she burst into tears.

Clara made it through the rest of the week by dogged determination. Sometimes she found herself thinking that she should check on Amos and Lily, only to remember it wasn't her job anymore.

Leah came by and left Clara the teaching guides, some back issues of *The Bulletin Board* and a complete set of the textbooks she would be teaching from throughout the year. It had been many years since Clara had studied history. It was never one of her strong subjects, so she spent hours poring over the course book she would be using. She was eager to begin her new job, but she was more eager for Sunday to arrive. Then, she would have the chance to ask Deborah Stutzman how the children were doing.

What she wouldn't be able to ask was how Ethan was doing. Her heart ached every time she thought of him.

When Sunday finally rolled around, she rushed

her family to get ready and get to the service early. Her efforts to be there before Deborah arrived were rewarded. She saw Deborah and her family getting out of their buggy and she went to help them unload the food they brought.

"Let me help you with that," she said as she took a carton of pies from Deborah's mother.

She stood aside to let Deborah's mother go first and fell into step beside the new nanny. "So, how was your first week with Ethan's children? Aren't Lily and Amos adorable?"

Deborah rolled her eyes. "That would depend on your definition of adorable. I don't know how you put up with them."

"They can be a little high-spirited, and Micah can be a handful, but they are good children."

"Your good children filled my new shoes full of maple syrup the first day I was there."

"How did they do that?"

"I took my shoes off because they were pinching my toes a little. You know how new shoes feel sometimes. When I went to put them back on to go home, they were full of syrup."

Clara struggled mightily not to laugh because it was clear that Deborah did not find it amusing. "Amos did that?"

"Lily did it. On the second day, someone put two big crickets in my purse. They nearly startled me to death when they jumped out. There is still one inside my buggy and its chirping is driving me nuts. I don't know which child did it. They won't tell."

They had reached the house, and Clara held the door for Deborah to go in. "I'm sorry they have been a trial for you, but things will get better. How is Micah?"

"He's no trouble at all. I hardly see him."

"And Ethan?" She tried to make the question sound casual, not as if she was dying to hear every detail about him.

They walked into the kitchen and began setting the food out to be served later. Deborah said, "He's fine, as far as I know. He goes to work. He comes home. I don't think he's said more than a dozen words to me. I know one thing for sure, he lets those children run wild. There is no discipline at all. I don't think they belong with a bachelor. I've talked to my uncle about it, and he believes I should bring it to the attention of their bishop. There has to be someone more suitable to raise them."

Clara's heart sank. "Ethan loves them. I'm sure with your help and guidance the children will straighten up and behave as they should."

"I'm not holding my breath. I'm looking for another position."

Clara spent the majority of the morning service praying for Ethan and the children. She was powerless to do anything else.

When the preaching was over and the meal had

been served, Clara took her plate and went to sit with her sisters on the lawn. Leah joined them a few minutes later. "Have you finished your history lessons, Clara?"

"I have."

"When was the Emancipation Proclamation signed?"

"January 1, 1863."

"Wait a minute," Betsy said. "If you're the teacher, why are you getting quizzed?"

"Because it's important for the teacher to stay ahead of her scholars," Leah answered.

Clara nodded. "In order to know more than they do, I have to study harder than they do."

Betsy shook her head. "I'm going to keep weaving baskets for Elam Sutter. It doesn't strain my brain."

"Is Sally upset that she didn't get the teaching job?" Leah took a bite of bread covered with peanut butter and molasses.

Betsy shook her head. "I don't know. She took a job as a nanny to an *Englisch* family. I heard she has moved in with them."

"She's living *Englisch?*" Leah covered her mouth with her hand. They were all shocked.

"That's what I heard, and she's not here today." Betsy bit into a brownie.

After a minute of stunned silence, Lizzie looked at Clara. "I saw you talking to Deborah Stutzman earlier. How is she getting along with Ethan and his children?"

"They filled her shoes full of syrup and put crickets in her purse."

Betsy spewed bits of brownie from her lips as she whooped with laughter. The women looked at each other and all started giggling. "It is a little funny," Clara admitted.

When Lizzie stopped laughing, she said, "Maybe we should find out if Ethan is looking for another replacement nanny."

Leah elbowed Clara. "You can ask him now. Here he comes."

After searching among the groups of churchgoers, Ethan finally located Clara sitting with a group of women on the lawn. She leaped to her feet and started toward him as soon as she caught sight of him.

"Ethan, what's wrong?"

He didn't question how she knew there was trouble. "Micah is missing. I told him to get ready for church this morning. He said he wasn't going, but I insisted. After I had Amos and Lily ready and fed, Micah still hadn't come down from his room. I went to check on him and he was gone. Amos and Lily say they don't know where he is. I've looked everywhere. I thought you might know where he would go."

She laid a hand on Ethan's arm. "I'm sure he's just hiding from you. He has done this before. He'll reappear when he is ready."

"That's what I thought until I realized Golda was missing, too. He's not hiding. He's taken the horse and run away."

Clara's eyes instantly filled with worry. "He couldn't possibly ride a horse that large by himself, could he?"

Ethan tried to hide his fear, but it wasn't easy. What if the boy had fallen off the mare? Without a saddle or harness to hold on to, he could easily slide off her broad back. He could be lying hurt somewhere and Ethan had no idea where to look.

"He's been riding since before he could walk. All he would need was a way to get up on her. Most likely, he used the fence. If he had something to tie to her halter to use as a rein, he could ride her anywhere. I followed Golda's tracks until they reached the blacktop. After that, I couldn't tell which way Micah took her. I drove several miles in both directions without seeing any sign of them. Then I came here. Think, Clara, has he ever mentioned somewhere he wanted to go? Someone he wanted to visit?"

"*Nee,* but it won't be hard to spot a horse that large. Where are Amos and Lily?"

"In my wagon."

She turned to the woman she had been talking

with. "Leah, we need to get up a search party for Ethan's nephew. He's gone missing."

Leah stepped toward them. "I heard. I'll get Caleb. He'll know what to do." She turned and hurried toward a group of men standing by the barn.

Ethan itched to be doing something, anything, but he had already done all he could think to do. "Micah is angry at God for taking his parents away. That's why he wouldn't go to church. I should have told him that I understand how he feels. Instead, I told him to stop acting like a baby."

"Don't blame yourself, Ethan. We will find him."

She sounded so certain. He wanted to believe her, but he couldn't summon the faith she had.

Leah returned with Caleb Mast and two teenage twin boys. Caleb held a cell phone. "I'm going to call 911. The sheriff's office can scour the roads much more quickly than we can by buggy."

He gestured toward the twins standing behind him. "This is Moses and Atlee Beachy. They have a couple of the fastest trotters in the county. They'll start from where you lost the boy's tracks and go in opposite directions along the highway. I want you to give all the details you have to the dispatcher. Are you ready?"

"*Ja.* I appreciate your help more than you can know."

Caleb gave a wry smile. "I've been in your shoes a time or two. Joy, my daughter, has Down syndrome. She used to run away all the time. Thankfully, it hasn't happened for a while."

Caleb placed the call and then gave Ethan the phone. He'd never used a cell phone before, but he managed not to drop it. When he finished talking to the sheriff's dispatcher, he handed the phone to Caleb. He had no idea how to turn it off.

"It's mine." One of the twins took it from him and slipped it in his pocket. The two boys took off.

Caleb said, "They both have phones. Like most Amish teenagers, they keep them out of sight because it upsets the adults. They'll call the sheriff and the phone shack closest to your house if they spot Micah. You should go home in case he is already there."

Ethan drew his hand over his face to ease his tense jaw muscles. "I guess you're right."

"Micah could be safe at home, unaware of the fuss he's set in motion and wondering where you are," Clara said softly.

Leah said, "We'll get some of the men here to start searching the roads and fields around your place. We'll find him."

Ethan prayed that was true. "Something tells me he's not at home, but I don't know where else to look."

Caleb laid a hand on Ethan's shoulder. "Take your other children home. I'm sure they're frightened."

Ethan gave in. He wasn't doing any good here. "All right."

"I'm coming with you. I can watch the little ones while you search. Let me tell my family and then I'll join you," Clara said.

He knew she would help no matter how things stood between them, and he was right.

He walked to his wagon. His horses were covered with flecks of foam and breathing fast. He'd pushed them hard this morning. They were used to pulling heavy loads for short distances, not racing across the countryside.

Adrian Lapp stopped him from climbing aboard the wagon. "Ethan, wait. I just heard what's going on. Take my horse and buggy. He's fresh and eager to get out on the highway. I can drive your team home slowly. My family and I aren't in any hurry."

"Are you sure?"

"Of course. It's the least I can do for my neighbor."

Clara came rushing to Ethan's side. "I'm ready."

"Clara!" Lily, who'd been huddled against Amos, brightened. "Micah is hiding again."

"I heard that. Are you sure that you don't know where he is?"

The children shook their heads.

"We're going to take Adrian's buggy." Ethan reached for Lily, and she came willingly. Clara lifted Amos down and they followed Adrian to the long line of buggies parked beside the road. His boy Kyle was already backing a black horse between the shafts. Ethan put Lily down and went to help finish the task.

After they were on their way at last, Ethan glanced at Clara. The children were exploring the backseat and bouncing on the cushions. "I haven't thanked you for coming along, Clara."

"You are welcome, but no thanks are needed."

Ethan couldn't think of anything else to say. He flicked the reins to keep the horse at a steady trot. At least the road was deserted on a Sunday morning and he didn't have to worry about traffic. He scanned the countryside and every lane hoping to catch a glimpse of a little boy on a big horse. "I just don't know what to do with that child."

"He's hurting and he doesn't know where to turn."

"He'll get over it, I know. It just takes time. But he has got to learn that he can't run away from problems."

"It's possible Micah is acting out because he has bottled up his anger and his grief. It's important that you talk to him about what's troubling him."

"I know he feels he needs to be the one taking care of his brother and sister. He resents that they had to come live with me."

"I don't think he resents you."

"I don't think he even likes me." He snapped reins again.

"Maybe he is afraid to like you," she suggested.

Puzzled, Ethan glanced at her. "Why would he be afraid to like me?"

"Because he doesn't want to feel the same kind of pain he's going through now if something should happen to you. He was so scared the night you cut your arm. You need to sit down and talk to him about the things he's afraid of. Losing you. Being alone. Being separated from his brother and sister."

They were the same kinds of fears that had plagued Ethan as a child, but he wasn't ready to admit that. "Let's pray that I have a chance to talk to him."

Clara laid a hand on his knee. "You will. Have faith, Ethan."

He swallowed against the tightness that closed his throat. Surely, God would not take Micah away from him, too.

Clara held on to her faith in God's goodness, but she couldn't stop worrying any more than Ethan could. Thankfully, the two younger children were soon dozing in the back of the buggy. Ethan kept the horse at a steady, ground-eating trot, but it still seemed to take forever to reach his lane. He pulled the buggy to a stop just beyond it and handed the reins to her while he jumped out to check the mese machine in the phone shack he shared with ner Amish families in the area.

He stepped inside the small gray-and-white building but came out almost instantly. He shook his head and her hopes fell. It didn't seem possible that a boy and a horse could vanish so completely. When Ethan climbed in beside her, she said, "Maybe he's waiting for you at home."

"Maybe."

There was nothing else to say. Ethan drove the buggy up the lane and stopped in front of the house. His mare whinnied from the pasture gate. Their borrowed horse answered her, waking the two children in the back. Lily sat up and rubbed her eyes. "Is Micah still lost? I want to see him."

"I'm hungry." Amos picked his hat up off the floor and put it on his head.

Ethan's gaze was fixed on his mare across the way. "Rosie is still alone in the pasture. I don't think Micah has come back."

Clara got down and opened the back door of the buggy. She lifted Lily out and then Amos. "Come inside, and I will fix you something for lunch."

Ethan got out and secured the horse. He began calling for Micah but got no answer. Clara said, "I'll check his room."

Ethan nodded. "If he's not here, I'm going back to the phone shack to wait for a call."

Clara had started to lead the children into the

house when the sound of a car coming up th
stopped her. She moved to stand by Ethan as
sheriff's white SUV stopped in front of them. T
tinted window rolled down. An officer in a brown trooper's hat pulled off his sunglasses. "Are you Ethan Gingerich?"

Ethan took a step forward. "I am."

The officer stepped out of the vehicle. "I'm Sheriff Nick Bradley. I understand that you have a missing child."

Clara moved up to grasp Ethan's arm. "His name is Micah. He's only eight years old. He's been missing since early this morning. He has blond hair and blue eyes. Ethan, what was he wearing?"

"Was he dressed like this?" Sheriff Bradley pulled open the rear door of his SUV. Micah sat slumped in the backseat with his eyes downcast.

With a glad cry, Clara raced toward him. Lily and Amos came right behind her. "Micah, you scared us all half to death. Are you all right?"

He nodded but didn't speak. He glanced toward his uncle. Clara realized Ethan was still standing by the porch steps. He was hanging on to the newel post as if he needed it to stay upright. He straightened when everyone looked his way and walked toward the vehicle. He stopped beside the sheriff. "You have my thanks for bringing him home safe. Where was he found?"

"He was at the bus station in Hope Springs.

...anted to trade his horse for a bus ticket to ...hart, Indiana."

Clara looked at Micah in amazement. They had people searching the roads and farms close by, but no one had thought to go into town to look for him.

"The horse was not his to trade," Ethan said.

The sheriff folded his arms. "I reckon that makes him a horse thief. The law is pretty tough on horse thieves. Do you want me to take him to jail?"

Clara stared at them in shock. "Ethan?" Amos and Lily were holding on to her skirt. They stared fearfully at the sheriff.

"I'm thinking on it." Ethan folded his arms and mimicked the sheriff's stance.

Aghast, Clara scowled at both of them. Now was no time to frighten the boy. She fumbled with the seat belt until she was able to release it. "Do not mind them, Micah."

"That has been the problem all along. He does not mind me, nor does he mind you. Perhaps he will mind Sheriff Bradley."

"I don't care if my prisoners mind me or not. I just lock them in a cell."

"You are not going to lock up this child. For shame, the both of you." Clara had Micah out of the car, but she kept a protective grip on his shoulders.

"Is my mare okay?" Ethan asked.

Micah turned and buried his face in Clara's

waist. How could Ethan be worried about his animal at a time like this?

Nick pushed his hat back with one finger. "As far as I could tell she is. Adrian Lapp has her. He's bringing her along with your other team."

Ethan shoved his hands in his pockets and rocked back on his heels. "I reckon the boy can stay here, then, if the *Englisch* law allows it."

"It allows some judgment calls on my part. You aren't going to be a repeat offender, are you, young man?"

Micah glanced his way from the safety of Clara's apron. "What does that mean?"

"Are you planning to borrow another horse without permission?"

"Nee."

"All right. He's all yours, Mr. Gingerich. Don't hesitate to call me if you change your mind." The sheriff tipped his hat toward Clara, got back in his SUV and drove away.

Ethan walked up to Micah with his hands on his hips. "It is time you and I had a long talk, Micah."

"Am I going to get a whipping now?" he asked fearfully.

Ethan dropped into a crouch, bringing him eye level with Micah. "No. I'm angry with you. I'm disappointed in you. But I'm so very thankful that you are safe."

Clara stepped back as he pulled the boy into his

arms. She pressed a hand to her lips to still their tremors as happiness and relief overwhelmed her. She couldn't tell which one of them needed the hug more. Perhaps now they could finally start being a real family.

As much as she wanted to be a part of that, she wasn't.

Chapter Thirteen

Clara watched Ethan release Micah and slowly rise to his feet. His eyes were bright with moisture when he looked her way. "Clara, would you be kind enough to fix the children something to eat."

"Of course."

"Micah and I will be in soon."

She nodded and took the little ones inside. "Go change out of your Sunday clothes while I find something to fix for lunch."

"Okay." Amos went upstairs.

Lily said, "Can we have cinnamon toast? *Mamm* used to make cinnamon toast on Sundays sometimes."

"That sounds like a fine idea. Go get changed, and you can help me fix it."

Clara glanced out the window but couldn't see Micah and Ethan. When Lily came downstairs, Clara took slices of bread and laid them on a cookie sheet. Mixing the sugar and the cinnamon together in a large shaker, she buttered the slices and gave the shaker to Lily. "Sprinkle it over the entire pan until it's gone. Try not to get too much on the floor."

Standing on a chair beside the kitchen table, Lily proceeded to shake the container as hard as she could. Most of it hit the bread, but a lot ended up on the tabletop.

Micah came in from outside. "*Onkel* Ethan said I should come get something to eat."

"Where is he?" Clara looked toward the door.

"He's taking care of the Lapps' horse." Micah licked his finger, ran it across the tabletop and popped his sugar-coated digit into his mouth.

Clara grinned and did the same.

"My *mamm* used to do that," he said.

"Lick the sugar and cinnamon off her fingers like this?" Clara made another swipe to demonstrate.

He grinned. "More like this." He licked his finger and made a big spiral through the sprinkles on the table before putting his finger back into his mouth.

Lily didn't bother with the tabletop. She pressed her hand on one of the slices of bread and licked her palm.

Clara glanced at Micah again. It was good that he could talk about his mother. She carried the bread to the oven and slipped it in. Casually, she asked, "What else do you remember about your mother, Micah?"

"I remember the way she laughed. I remember the way she would kiss my forehead when I finished my prayers and she tucked me in at night."

"I remember that, too," Lily said.

"Remember what?" Amos asked as he came in.

"Lily and Micah were telling me some of the things they remember about your mother."

"I remember that she made the best fried chicken," he said.

"And apple pie in a brown paper bag." Micah took a seat at the table. Amos came and sat beside him. Both boys continued to clean up the spilled cinnamon sugar.

Micah folded his arms on the table and rested his chin on them. "She loved pickled beets. She always offered me some when she opened a jar. I always told her no because I don't like them. She would laugh and say, 'All the more for me.' I miss her laugh. I wish I liked pickled beets."

Clara heard the screen door open. She glanced that way and saw Ethan come in. The children hadn't noticed. She held a finger to her lips. Ethan gave her a funny look but stood still.

"What else do you remember, Lily?"

Lily touched her *kapp*. "*Mamm* used to brush my hair and sing a song for me. *Onkel* Ethan brushes my hair now, but he doesn't do it right. He pulls on the tangles, and he doesn't sing."

"She liked to sing," Amos said. "She told *Daed* that he sounded like a bullfrog when he tried to sing."

"*Ja,* like the bullfrog I caught in the creek." Lily picked up the shaker, poured some of the mixture into her palm and licked it.

Micah looked at Clara. There were tears in his eyes. "I wish I could remember her face better. Sometimes I can't see it."

Her heart twisted with empathy when she saw the pain on his face. She wanted so much to help him.

"I see her face every time I look at Lily," Ethan said from the doorway.

The children all looked his way. Micah wiped his tears away and put his head down.

Lily touched her face. "I look like *Mamm?*"

Ethan came to the table and sat down beside Lily. "You look a lot like her. You have her eyes and her nose. You have her smile, too. Amos, you are going to have your *daed's* big feet. You for sure have his ears." The boy grinned and put his hands over them.

"What do I have?" Micah asked, but he didn't look at Ethan.

"You have your father's heart. I see all the love

he had for his family in you. You have his eyes and his short temper."

That made Micah look up. "*Daed* didn't have a temper."

"When he was your age he sure did. He hit me in the mouth and knocked out my front tooth when I was seven and he was six. He got a spanking from our *daed* for that."

"What did you do to make him mad?" Clara asked, so happy for them all that she thought she might cry. This sharing was what they needed. Grief had its time, but good memories would last forever.

"I broke his scooter. It was an accident, but he didn't see it that way. He never was scared of me even though I was older and bigger. After he met your mother, Micah, I never saw him lose his temper again. He loved her so much." Ethan wiped his eyes with his shirtsleeve.

Micah's lip quivered, but he said, "He loved you, too. He used to talk about you a lot after you moved away. He missed you. Why did you leave?"

Ethan rose to his feet and crossed to the open door. "For a foolish reason. I know that now. I wish I had stayed and worked with him the way we always planned. Lily, I'm sorry I pull your hair. I'll be more careful from now on."

"That's okay. Clara does it nice. I like it when you're with us, Clara. I don't miss *Mamm* so much when you're here. I wish you could stay for always. I'm gonna ask God if He can do that."

Clara couldn't speak past the lump in her throat. She couldn't look at Ethan or he would see how much she wished for exactly the same thing. Any doubts she had about her feelings for Ethan vanished. She loved him. And his children.

"How else am I like *Daed?*" Amos asked.

Ethan rejoined them at the table. "Your dad was scared of bees."

"I'm not scared of bees." Amos puffed out his chest.

"You are, too," Lily said. Amos scowled at her.

"Everyone is afraid of something. Clara is afraid of big horses. Micah is afraid of something, too. What is that, Micah?"

"I don't know." The boy looked down.

Clara said, "When my parents died, I was afraid that I wouldn't be able to take care of my sisters. I was the oldest, so I knew it was my responsibility. What were you going to do when you got back to Indiana, Micah?"

"Go home."

"Someone else lives there now," Ethan said gently.

"I know. I was going to see Mr. Danny. He told me when I was big enough he'd give me a job in his sawmill."

Clara saw his reasoning. "So you would have a

way to take care of your brother and sister if something bad happened to your *onkel* Ethan."

Micah looked up at Ethan with tears flowing unchecked down his face. "A widow-maker might get you, and if you aren't here anymore, the old aunts could take Lily and Amos away. God took *Mamm* and *Daed* away for no reason. He could take you, too."

Ethan gathered the boy into his arms. Micah clung to him and sobbed as if his heart was breaking. "You don't have to worry, Micah. You don't have to be the strong one and try to do it alone. I'm going to make sure you kids stay together. I'm going to make sure there is someone to take care of you if I can't."

Clara stroked his hair. "To be Amish is to care for one another. If need be, there are many families in this community that will make a place for all of you. My family would take you in. Adrian Lapp and his family would take you in. You are not alone here unless you choose to be. You blame God, but His ways are beyond our understanding. You mother and father are with Him and with each other. Their love for you has not died. It shines strongest when you love and care for each other."

Ethan cast her a look filled with gratitude and something else. Was it affection she saw shining in his eyes? Or was she only seeing what she wanted to see?

She turned away and pulled the toast from the oven before she made a fool of herself and told him how much she had come to care for him.

When she had her emotions under control, she carried the tray of bread to the table. Ethan was drying Micah's eyes on his shirtsleeve. Lily and Amos were watching their brother with worried faces. Clara hugged them both. "It's going to be all right now."

Ethan nodded. "I think you're right. I think we're going to be okay. What do you think, Micah?"

He sniffed and said, "I think so, too. Can I have some cinnamon toast now?"

Ruffling the boy's hair, Ethan said, "You can have all you want."

The children finished eating just as the Lapp family arrived with the wagon. Ethan went out to greet them.

After Adrian transferred his family to his buggy, he came to Clara, who was waiting on the porch. "Ethan and I have talked it over. I'll take Faith and the baby home, then I'll be back to take you home."

"You don't have to do that. I can walk."

"My wife will have my hide if I don't take you, and you know how she can be."

"All right. I'll wait for you here."

"*Goot.* I'll be back in twenty minutes."

Clara could have insisted on riding with them now, but her foolish heart wasn't ready to leave.

She wanted a little more time with Ethan. She was waiting on the porch for him when he came back from putting his horses up.

He took a seat on the railing the way Micah often did. "Thanks again for your help. You dropped everything to help, even after the way I spoke to you last week."

"It's forgiven and forgotten." Yet it wasn't. She could tell by the guarded look in his eyes. Was it her broken engagement that troubled him or was it something else?

They sat in awkward silence until Adrian Lapp returned. Clara rose and grasped at one last straw to see Ethan again.

"My family and some of our friends are having a picnic at the lake on Thursday. We're celebrating Naomi's birthday with a surprise get-together. You and your family are welcome to come. You and the boys can bring your fishing poles."

She held her breath as she waited for his answer and tried not to get her hopes up. Ethan wouldn't look at her. "I never cared much for fishing."

Her hopes fell. "I see."

She started to leave, but his voice stopped her. "It would be fun for the children, though."

"It would. There will be other children there for them to play with."

"Thanks for the invitation." He turned around.

The warmth she had come to treasure was missing from his eyes.

"Does that mean you will come?" She held her breath.

"I can't promise anything, but I'll try."

Ethan drew the wagon to a halt in the shade of an element tree beside the lake in Woolly Joe's pasture on Thursday afternoon. Half a dozen buggies and three farm wagons were already there ahead of him. He saw a number of women seated on quilts near the shore. Four older girls in dark blue dresses and white bonnets held their skirts hiked to their knees as they waded a few feet out into the lake. He recognized Clara among them. He'd spent two long sleepless nights trying to come to grips about his feelings for her. He was no closer to resolving them than he had been the day she left his house.

The women were laughing and splashing each other by kicking the water in wide arcs that sparkled in the sunlight. Farther down the shoreline were men with fishing poles casting out into the water. He saw only one woman with a pole in her hand and recognized Joann Weaver, a woman who worked at the printing company. He had met her before when he placed an ad for his business in the paper. She saw him and lifted a hand to wave at the same time the tip dipped. She quickly began to reel in her catch.

Kyle Lapp came racing up to the wagon. He was wearing only a pair of wet pants held up by his suspenders. His red hair was plastered to his head. It was apparent he had already been in the water. "Hi, Micah, do you want to come and try our rope swing? My uncle Ben rigged it for us and it works great."

Micah looked at Ethan. "Can I?"

The boy had changed drastically since his aborted attempt to run away. He was no longer brooding and moody, but a joy to be around with a quick wit and a ready smile. It would be good for him to have fun with boys his own age. Ethan nodded. "Sure, as long as there is an adult present."

"My uncle Ben is there and so are Atlee and Moses."

"Okay. Leave your shirt here, Micah. You brought dry clothes to change into, didn't you?"

Micah was already peeling off a shirt. "I did."

He jumped down from the wagon and headed up the shoreline with Kyle. Amos asked, "Can I go play on the rope swing?"

"I think you're too small yet. You should stay with Lily and me."

Clara approached his wagon with a wary look in her eyes. He knew a stab of guilt. He missed the warmth that used to fill her gaze when she looked at him. She said, "I'm glad you decided to come."

He handed Lily down to her. "You look like

you were having fun." The hem of her dress was soaked, and there were damp spots sprinkled across the fabric.

"I was. Lily, would you like to go wading with us?"

"Can I?" Lily looked to Ethan.

"She will be fine with me," Clara reassured him.

"I know she will." Some of the tension left his body. She truly cared about his children. Was he wrong about her? Was she a woman of honor in spite of breaking her vow to wed? He wanted to believe she was.

"Amos, would you like to join us?" she asked.

"Sure." The children scampered down.

Clara took them to introduce them to Naomi, who was surrounded by friends and family and holding her new grandbaby. Ethan unharnessed the horses and staked them out to graze, then he joined Joe and Carl King at the edge of the lake. "If you don't like crowds, Joe, how did this happen?"

"My granddaughters dreamed it up. Naomi is happiest with folks around her. Never forget that a happy wife makes for a happy life."

Ethan and Carl shared an amused glance. Joe didn't look all that happy.

Joe scratched his beard. "Ethan, you were right about the price of the walnut wood. I made a tidy profit on the few you took in. Would you like to take a look at another grove of timber for me?"

"Sure. I have time now."

"Carl, why don't you take him up there. You know the spot I mean."

Carl led the way and Ethan followed to the opposite side of the lake. After about ten minutes of walking, they entered a narrow ravine similar to the one Ethan had logged out earlier. A bare trickle of water ran along the bottom, but the sides were steeper.

"Will it be a problem to get your horses in here?" Carl asked.

"Not to this point, but let's see how much steeper it gets up ahead."

They followed the ravine to where the trees closed in on either side of the high bank. Just beyond the narrow place, it widened out into a sloping meadow studded with tall walnut trees. "I think this is where Joe had in mind," Carl said.

Ethan walked around the largest tree, studying the lay of the land and how close the other trees were to it. He flexed his sore arm. "It's a nice stand. I count fifteen of these big fellows. I can cut them, but I'll need to widen a trail to haul them out over that narrow spot."

"I'll help you with that."

Ethan looked at him in surprise. "*Danki,* it will make the work go faster and smoother."

"I worked as a logger for a while. Before I became a shepherd."

"Which is easier?" Ethan asked with a grin.

"You'd think sheep, but I say logging."

"There's at least five days of work here. Do I talk price with you, or with Joe?" Ethan asked.

"With Joe."

"All right. We should get back to the party before all the food is gone."

"Lizzie and her sisters brought enough food to feed us for a week. You don't need to worry that they will run out."

"You haven't seen how my nephew Micah can pack it away." The two men started back down the ravine. "Clara mentioned that you and Lizzie planned to wed in the fall."

"Did she sound happy about it?" Carl asked.

It was an odd question, but Ethan told the truth. "She said she wasn't certain it was the right thing for Lizzie."

"She is not certain that I'm the right man for Lizzie or that any man would be the right man. Clara has a poor opinion of marriage."

"I heard she was engaged, but she changed her mind at the last minute and moved here. Some women think there is better to be had. A pledge to marry is not something to be discarded. She didn't strike me as a fickle woman, but I've been wrong before."

Carl looked shocked. "Did Clara tell you about her broken engagement?"

"*Nee,* it was someone else who mentioned it."

Carl was quiet for a moment. Then he said, "After their parents died, the girls went to live with their *onkel.* He was an abusive man."

"Clara mentioned that."

Carl looked surprised. "Did she?"

"She was worried that I might be unkind to my niece and nephews."

"That makes sense. The family lived in Indiana on a dairy farm owned by a man named Rufus Kuhns. He is a bad apple, a man truly in need of our prayers. Even though he is more than sixty years old, he decided he wanted Clara to be his wife. He had been widowed twice before. She didn't want to marry him."

"I suppose she was in love with someone else."

"No, there wasn't anyone else. Clara suspected what kind of man he was. Rufus told Clara if she wouldn't marry him, he'd wed Betsy, the youngest. He threatened to evict all of them from their home. Under pressure from her *onkel,* Clara gave in and agreed."

"Are you serious?" Ethan had never heard of such a thing from an Amish family.

"It was much worse than that, and Clara bore the brunt of it."

Ethan stiffened and looked at Carl. "What are you saying?"

"I saw Rufus strike her across the face in front of

her whole family. Sadly, Lizzie told me it wasn't the first time. What he would do in private I hesitate to think about. Clara won't talk about it. She has been painfully shy since I met her, but she has started to open up since she began working for you."

"She loves the children," Ethan said quickly. He tried to digest this new information about her. He had wronged her by assuming her reason for ending her engagement was trivial. Just as she assumed he might be like her uncle, he assumed she was like Jenny. What a fool he was. He should've known better.

All the signs of Jenny's discontent had been right in front of his face. He had refused to see them because he wanted her as his wife. Clara wasn't discontent. She knew how to make do, she knew how to entertain the children and she enjoyed the little things of life that meant so much to all of them.

Carl cleared his throat. "I've told you these things because I didn't want you to have the wrong idea about Clara. She is a good woman, and she will make a fine teacher."

"*Ja,* she will," Ethan admitted although it saddened him that she wasn't working for him anymore. He owed her an apology. He prayed it would be enough to mend their friendship.

Clara enjoyed her afternoon with Amos and Lily, but it was bittersweet because she knew these kinds of days would be few and far between in the future. Micah was racing about with Kyle and some of his friends, looking like a boy without a care in the world. If nothing else, her time with Ethan and his family had allowed her to help the troubled boy.

It was a busy and fun-filled day. She often caught sight of Ethan watching her, but he never spoke to her. The day drew to a close at last. She walked a ways along the lakeshore in search of a moment of peace and quiet.

"Clara, I'd like to speak to you."

She turned to see Ethan had followed her. "It's getting late. I should be going."

She moved away from him although what she wanted was to move closer. She wanted to feel his arms around her. She wanted to know if he thought she was pretty.

Silly thought.

Vain thought.

"Please, I only need a few minutes of your time. I owe you an apology."

Her gaze flew to his face. "Why?"

"Walk with me for a little bit, please?"

She glanced at her family gathering up the blankets and basket. Ethan's children were with Faith Lapp. Clara wasn't needed. "All right."

The heat of the day had given way to a cool evening breeze. High white wisps of clouds patterned the sky. "Mares' manes and mares' tails,"

Ethan said. "It means rain in a few days. We could use some to green up the pasture. My *fuah* would enjoy that."

He was always thinking about his fearsome team of horses. "It would be nice if it rained and settled the dust."

They began walking along the lakeshore away from the group. The silence lengthened until they rounded a bend in the trail and were out of sight of the others. He said, "Carl King told me about the man you were to marry."

"He shouldn't have done that." She kept walking.

"I'm sorry that you were placed in such a terrible situation. I'm sorry, too, that I assumed you had broken the engagement because you were a fickle woman who wanted something better."

"I did want something better." She hated talking about that time of her life.

"Clara, you do deserve something better. I judged too harshly." There was remorse in his tone and something else. Sadness? Regret?

She glanced at him from the corner of her eye. "You judged me harshly because the woman you wanted to marry chose to marry another?"

He stopped walking. "Where did you hear that?"

She stopped, too. "Micah once mentioned that was the reason you moved here."

Ethan started walking again. She fell into step beside him. He was silent for so long that she thought the conversation was over. She stopped walking and laid a hand on his arm. “I’m still your friend. If it would help to talk about it, I’m listening.”

Chapter Fourteen

Ethan stared straight ahead. He normally kept his emotions under tight control. He didn't discuss his past or share the details with anyone, but something in Clara's kind and sympathetic words opened the door he'd kept shut for so long.

"When I was ten years old, my mother chose to leave our family, and our Amish faith, but she didn't go alone. She took Greg with her. It was years before I saw him again."

"Oh, Ethan. I'm so sorry. Why did she leave?"

Hadn't he asked himself that question a million times? Even today, he didn't have an answer that soothed the hurt.

"I'm not sure. My father never spoke about it. It was as if she never existed after she was gone. My aunts once said it was because she had a mental breakdown. From what Greg told me of his time with her, I think my aunts were right. At least she wanted one of us." He still wondered why she took only Greg. Why didn't she want him, too?

Clara laid a hand on his arm. Her comforting touch gave him the confidence to go on. "The years I spent with my father after that were lonely ones. He never complained, but the joy went out of his eyes. He grew old so quickly. Because we lived in a tiny rural community, I had to attend a public school with only three other Amish children, all girls. If it hadn't been for Danny McCurdy, a friendly *Englisch* boy who appointed himself my defender from the school bullies, it would have been intolerable. We were an odd pair, but Danny and I became close friends. I never forgot about my brother, though."

"Of course not," Clara said.

It was difficult to talk about that time in his life, but Ethan drew strength from Clara's understanding. "Greg never forgot about me, either. When he turned eighteen and Mother couldn't stop him, he returned to us and took up the Amish life again. I was never so glad to see anyone. It was as if the years had only been days. The two of us picked up right where we left off. There were some rough spots, but we were together again. Greg quickly became friends with Danny. The three of us had some great times together."

"And your mother?" Clara asked quietly.

"She didn't return. She lives in Indianapolis now, the last I heard."

"How sad, but I'm sure your father was happy to have both his sons with him again."

"He was. Greg was eager to learn the logging trade and work beside us. Some of the joy returned to my father's eyes, but only for a while. He grew pale and thin over the next winter. He refused to see a doctor in spite of our urging. One day, he didn't wake up."

"You have seen more than your share of sorrow, Ethan, but the Lord is with you. He can be your strength as He has been mine."

It was what he was supposed to do, rely on the Lord, but he was finding it hard. When Clara spoke again, she asked, "Why did you move so far away from your brother and his family? It sounds as if you were very close."

"We were close, but it wasn't long after Greg returned that he met and married an Amish girl named Mary. Our community was growing by then with more Amish families moving into the area. Mary was as sweet as they come. Micah was born the next year. Amos and Lily came along in due time. My brother seemed to have a blessed life. For me, it wasn't like that. It was six more years before the woman I wanted to marry moved to our town."

He had craved the joy he saw in his brother's face whenever he looked at Mary and his children. To be included in a whole and loving family, Ethan wanted that, too. A family and a woman to make his house a home. Someone to love him unconditionally. When he met Jenny, he thought he'd found it. But she had cast aside his love just as his mother had. What was wrong with him?

Clara looked away from him. Ethan caught the change that came over her face and wondered at it. She crossed her arms. "Who was she?"

"Her name was Jenny. We courted, I proposed, she accepted me over a half-dozen other fellows. I was on top of the world. Then I introduced her to my friend Danny." His joy turned to ashes within a few short months.

"Didn't they get along?"

"That wasn't the problem. I thought we were all going to be friends. I didn't see it was becoming something more between them until the day she told me she intended to marry Danny instead of me."

"She left the Amish?"

"*Ja.* She said she wanted a better life than I could give her. A more comfortable life and Danny could give her that. Danny and his father owned the sawmill and lumberyard in our town. I couldn't avoid seeing them together week after week. Each time it was like fresh salt in the wound. I became a bitter man. It was my brother who suggested I leave and start over somewhere else."

"So you came here because of them?"

"Foolish, wasn't it?"

"I don't think so. Have you forgiven them?" Clara asked softly.

They had to live their lives and he had to go on with his. He had misjudged Clara; perhaps he had misjudged Jenny, too, and she did love Danny. Only God could see into the hearts of men and women. It was time to let go of the bitterness that had ruled his life.

Ethan smiled at Clara. "I have."

"Then you have done as our Lord commands. He must be very pleased with you."

What Ethan wanted was for Clara to be pleased with him. "Have you forgiven you fiancé for his cruelty?"

The animation vanished from her face. She stared at the ground. "I have."

"Perhaps another man can erase the cruel memories you bear."

"I don't see how."

"So you never plan to marry?" He watched her expression closely.

She put her hands in her apron pockets and started walking back the way they had come. She didn't look at him. "God has chosen the life of a teacher for me. I'm more than content with that. I don't need anything else."

"What about companionship, children?"

"I will have a school full of children and I have you, my friend, and my family for companionship. It is a full life. Do not feel sorry for me."

"I would never feel sorry for you, Clara. I will cherish your friendship always. I'm going to be cutting some more lumber for your grandfather starting on Monday. What would you think about my bringing the children to stay with you while I'm doing that?"

She stopped and looked at him with a bright smile. "I would love that, but what about Deborah?"

"She isn't working out."

"I'm sorry. I hoped she would."

"You're a hard woman to replace, Clara." How was he going to manage without her in his life?

Ethan poured himself, Micah and Carl King a glass of lemonade and set the pitcher on the table at Joe's house. They were all thirsty after clearing brush that morning. Rain had put a stop to their work for the time being. Both men took a seat at the table, and Micah carried his glass out onto the porch, where Clara was sitting with the other children.

Ethan drummed the tabletop with his fingers as he stared out the window at the curtain of rain obscuring the sheep pens and barns.

"You look deep in thought, Ethan. Is something wrong, besides the weather?" Carl asked.

"I had a letter from my aunts yesterday."

"Bad news?" Carl asked.

"You could say that. They are coming for a visit."

"How is that bad news?"

"They want to take two of the children back with them."

"Are you serious? Why now?"

"It appears my unhappy nanny spoke to my bishop about how undisciplined and wild I have allowed the children to become."

"I heard about the syrup in her shoes. That's funny."

"Only if it isn't your shoes. My bishop contacted the bishop where the children are from and he, in turn, contacted my aunts. I'm still having trouble believing it. They intend to enlist the aid of my bishop to convince me to let Amos and Lily go home with them. My aunts can be very tenacious when they have a mission. You know what that means."

"Shunning, if you don't go along with what your church says. Been there, done that, as the *Englisch* say. The children are inventive, but I wouldn't call them undisciplined. They simply like Clara. You aren't going to let them go, are you?"

Ethan paced across the kitchen and then back. "I don't know what to do. I don't have a nanny, and Clara won't be able to keep them after this week. Maybe my aunts are right. Maybe I need to let them take the younger children, at least until they are old enough to start school. Then they can come back."

"I know what would solve your problem."

Ethan looked hopefully at his friend. "What?"

"You need a wife."

Ethan's mouth dropped open. "And you think that would be easier than finding a nanny?"

"Clara is single. The two of you get along pretty well from what I've seen."

Ethan shook his head. "She wouldn't have me. Besides, I have no wish to marry." His usual assertion sounded hollow this time.

"Marriage would solve all your problems."

"Make new ones, you mean." Ethan walked to the door and looked out the screen. Clara was seated on a chair at the end of the porch. Lily was in her lap. Amos sat cross-legged in front of her while Micah perched on the porch railing nearby moving his hand through the streams of water coursing off the roof. Clara was reading them a story. They were enthralled with her animated voice and hung on her every word.

They looked so right together. Like a mother with her children gathered around her. If only she were their mother. She would do anything for them, but would she marry to keep them together?

Carl left the table and came to stand beside Ethan. He clapped him on the shoulder. Ethan flinched. His arm was better but not fully healed. "Are we calling it quits for the day?"

"*Ja*. I won't work my team in the rain. It's too dangerous."

Carl leaned closer. "She likes you. More than a little. I can see that you like her, too. It's something to think about, my friend." He went out the door and waved to Clara before he dashed across the yard to the sheep barn.

Marriage for the sake of the children? Would she do it? Ethan had seen the aversion that filled her eyes at the mention of marriage. Was there a way to keep this lovely gentle woman in his children's lives and keep them united? The children thrived under her care. He saw the love she had for them, and they for her.

What if he promised her a marriage in name only? Their friendship would be a good foundation to build upon and the situation might not frighten her as much. Over time, her fear of intimacy would lessen and the future would take care of itself. It just might work.

Lily saw him at the doorway and motioned for him to come closer. "Come listen to the story with us."

He walked out onto the porch. "I have work to do."

Lily slipped off Clara's lap. She padded across to him and took his hand. "You can work after the story is done. It won't take long. Please?"

Ethan foresaw years of giving in to Lily's winsome ways. It took a harder man than he was to resist the pleading in her big eyes. He swung her up into his arms. "All right. But just one story."

He settled in the empty chair beside Clara. Lily stayed in his lap with her arm around his neck. He didn't pay much attention to the story, but he enjoyed the sound of Clara's voice and watching her expressive face. It was easy to imagine that this was how Greg and Mary must have felt when they were together with the children. Ethan hadn't realized how desperately he wanted to form a family of his own until this very moment. A family with Clara at its center.

He'd given up thoughts of marriage after Jenny, but Carl had planted the idea in Ethan's brain and it wouldn't go away. Clara was single. She wasn't averse to him. They got along well enough. More than well enough. They had a true friendship. He knew about the horror of her previous engagement. Convincing her to marry him would not be easy, but it just might be possible.

Clara wasn't sure she had ever known such happiness. Surrounded by the children she had grown to love and seated beside the man who made her heart beat faster every time he looked at her—no, she had never been happier. She read the story slowly, embellishing it, drawing it out, because she didn't want the story to end.

She glanced at Ethan and found him watching

her with a strange expression on his face. Did he know that she was falling in love with him? He was such a kind man. She never expected to feel like this about anyone. How had it happened to her? She had only known him a short time, but that didn't matter. Time and again, he had proved himself to be a man she could respect and admire.

But were her affections returned? That was what she really wanted to know, but it wasn't something she could ask him. They had developed a wonderful friendship with the children at the center of it. Would that friendship grow into something more over time, or would it wither and die once she began teaching school and wasn't here to see him every day?

She had prayed so hard that God would grant her the opportunity to teach school. Now that He had answered her prayers, she was ashamed to admit that it wasn't what she wanted after all. But was it what she was meant to do? Or was she meant to stay and care for these children?

As all things must, the story came to an end. She closed the pages of the book.

"Can you read us another one?" Lily asked.

"Nee," Ethan said. "There is work to be done at home since I can't log. Get your coats and umbrellas and I'll bring the wagon around.

The children left, but Ethan remained. "Clara,

I wondered if you would be free to drive out with me on Sunday evening?"

That sounded so much like an invitation for a date that she was sure she'd heard him wrong "I'm sorry. Did you ask me to go with you on Sunday evening? Are you taking the children somewhere?"

He looked vaguely uncomfortable. "I just wanted to go for a drive with you."

She hadn't heard wrong. He was asking her out.

Joy bubbled through her veins and made her smile. Just as quickly, she realized she might be reading too much into his request. She nodded, not trusting herself to speak without giggling.

"*Goot.* I'll pick you up at five."

"What will we do with the children?"

"Will one of your sisters watch them?"

"I'll ask."

The children returned in short order, and Ethan and his family left as the rain began to taper off. Once the wagon was out of sight, Clara threw her arms wide and spun in a happy circle. She had a date with Ethan.

If she expected Ethan's behavior to be different the next day, she was disappointed. He was as friendly as ever, but there wasn't anything special in the way he looked at her or in the way he spoke to her. She began to wonder if she was mistaken about his intentions. Perhaps he only wanted to talk to her about her position with the school. If he asked her to give up the teaching job and remain as the children's nanny, would she do it?

While it might be what she wanted, she had already made a commitment to the school board. To back out now would cause problems for everyone involved. Could they even find another teacher on such short notice? Both Sally and Deborah had other jobs. Only Melinda Miller was still looking. Would the board even hire her after turning her down once?

Clara prayed for guidance and focused her attention on the children who needed her today, but Sunday couldn't come soon enough.

When the much anticipated day finally arrived, Clara endured considerable teasing from Greta and Betsy when they learned she was going out. But Lizzie was totally on her side.

"There is nothing wrong with Clara going out for a drive on a Sunday afternoon," Lizzie said. "I'll be going out for a drive with Carl."

Betsy sank onto Clara's bed and propped her chin in her hands. "That is old news. You two have been driving out every Sunday for months. Greta and I are going to the singing together tonight, but don't expect us to come home together."

"Why wouldn't we come home together?" Greta asked.

Betsy rolled over to grin at her sister. "Because someone else will be driving me home. Again."

"Who?" Greta demanded. Clara was glad not to be the focus of their attention for a change.

"You'll see." Betsy rose and began to change her dress.

Greta crossed her arms and glared at all of her sisters. "This isn't fair. Why am I the only one without a boyfriend?"

"Ethan is not my boyfriend," Clara said quickly.

"Sounds like he is to me." Greta smoothed the wrinkles from her apron and straightened her *kapp.*

Lizzie gave Clara a quick hug. "He might not be your boyfriend yet, but give him a chance."

Clara looked down at her hands clasped together in her lap. "It feels strange."

"What does?" Betsy asked.

"Not being afraid to be alone with a man." She didn't want to think about Rufus, but she couldn't block out his face.

All of her sisters gathered around her. Lizzie said, "No one deserves to be happy as much as you do. You took care of us after *Mamm* died. You were willing to marry that horrid man so that none of us had to. If Ethan Gingerich doesn't know how blessed he is to have you in his life, then he is a fool."

"Thank you, all of you. You are absolutely the best sisters in the world. I hope that I'm not imagining that he likes me. I'll be mortified if this outing is to talk about my job."

From her seat by the window, Greta said, "You'll get to find out soon enough. He's here. He has the prettiest horses."

"Did he drive those big things?" Clara suppressed a shudder.

"Yup."

"It doesn't matter what he is driving," Lizzie said. "Go down and have a good time."

Clara was too nervous to have a good time, but she hugged her sister anyway and went downstairs. Ethan was already at the door. Her grandfather and Naomi were seated in the living room. Naomi had agreed to watch Ethan's children for a while and welcomed them warmly. Her grandfather didn't say anything—he simply went back to reading his paper. She wondered what he thought about her going out with Ethan, but knew he wouldn't voice an opinion unless she asked.

"Good afternoon, Clara." Ethan looked very handsome in his dark vest, bright white shirt and dark felt hat. It was the first time she had seen him in anything other than his work clothes. She noticed a button was missing on his vest. She would fix that soon.

It was such a wifely thought that she blushed.

"I thought we might take a drive out to the lake."

"That sounds nice."

He led the way to his wagon and helped her in.

"I hope you don't mind riding in the wagon. I've been meaning to get a new buggy."

"This is fine," she said, trying not to look at the massive animals in front of her.

He climbed up beside her and spoke to the horses. They moved out at a steady walk. When they reached a shady spot beside the water, he said, "Whoa." The horses stopped immediately.

"They are a well-trained pair," she said as Ethan helped her down from the wagon.

He walked up to pat Dutch on his muscular neck. Clara moved away. Ethan said, "They are a *goot fuah,* a good team. I trained them myself. Hopefully, I can buy more horses to train next spring. Cutting trees will take me away from the children too much in the fall and winter. I love my work. I love being in the woods and working with these horses, but I know I have to do what is best for the children."

"I understand and I respect that."

"I knew you would. Clara…I wanted to talk to you about something."

"Okay."

He began walking away from the wagon and she followed. Somehow, this wasn't feeling like a date.

"My aunts are coming to visit and they want to take Lily and Amos back with them. They intend to convince my bishop it's the right thing to do for the children."

"But it isn't! Do you want me to speak to him or to your aunts? I will."

He turned to face her and took her hands between his. "I know you love them as I do, and you would do almost anything for them."

"I would. You can't let them be split up. It will crush Micah."

"There's an answer to this problem, but I need your help. I want you to think about this carefully before you answer. Clara, we are friends. As a friend, I'm asking you to marry me."

"What?" She drew back in confusion.

"I know of your aversion to marriage. I assure you that our union will be in name only until you say otherwise. I will care and provide for you all your life and seek to make you happy no matter what else happens or doesn't happen between us. You can be the children's mother. You can be with them every day, help them grow in life and in their faith. You are the perfect woman for the job. They already love you."

The children loved her, but Ethan couldn't say that he loved her.

Because he didn't.

A marriage in name only. A safe and secure life with the children, but with a man who didn't love her.

She couldn't do it. Not even for the children. She couldn't tie herself into a loveless marriage. She had escaped such a prison once. She would not venture there again.

"I'm sorry, Ethan, but my answer is no." She pulled her hands away from him and started toward the wagon. "Please take me home."

"But why, Clara? Isn't this what you want? Children and a home of your own?"

"If I ever marry, it will be a real marriage, not some sham. Take me home." Before she burst into tears and made a bigger fool of herself than she already had.

Chapter Fifteen

How could it have gone so horribly wrong? Ethan glanced again at Clara sitting bolt upright beside him on the wagon seat. She wouldn't even speak to him. She sat with her eyes straight ahead, and her trembling lower lip clenched between her teeth. As they rumbled into the yard, he saw Carl was helping Lizzie into his buggy.

Lizzie smiled and waved. Clara jumped off the wagon and ran into the house. Lizzie's eyes grew wide. She said something to Carl and then followed Clara into the house.

Carl ambled over to Ethan. "That was a short date."

"I wouldn't call it a date. She hates me now and it's all your fault."

Carl clapped a hand to his chest. "My fault. What did I do?"

"You told me to propose to her."

"You seriously sprang the big question on your first date?"

Ethan pulled his hat off and ran his hands through his hair. "I'm short on time."

Lizzie came marching out of the house and stopped by Carl. She glared at Ethan with her hands on her hips. "I told my sister that if you didn't know what a treasure she was that you were a fool. I had no idea how big a fool you actually are. Carl, I'm sorry but I have had a change of plans this evening. I have to stay home and comfort my broken-hearted sister."

She marched back into the house, leaving Carl with a stunned look on his face. "What did you say to Clara? A speech about undying love doesn't generally turn out so badly."

"I left that part out." His well-thought-out plan had blown up in his face.

Carl gaped at him. "Seriously? You asked a woman to marry you and neglected to mention how much you love her?"

"I offered her a marriage in name only. I thought she would feel safe if I did that. I thought she would marry me because she loved the children, not because she loved me."

"All signs point to the fact that you thought wrong." Pushing away from the wagon, Carl tucked his hands in his pockets and gazed at the sky.

Heavy clouds were rolling in. "Looks like we're in for more rain."

The front door of the house opened and Naomi stepped out onto the porch with her arms crossed and a deep scowl on her face. "The children would like to spend the night with us, Ethan. You should go home now."

Carl backed away and said quietly, "Mama Bear has spoken. I would get while the getting's good if I were you. See you tomorrow if the rain lets up."

Ethan took the hint and drove home alone. He had made a mess of it. A complete mess of it. He had alienated the woman he loved with all his heart, and her family, too. Why hadn't he realized how much he cared for her before he proposed? "Please, Lord. How can I make this right?"

With a crack of thunder, the sky opened up and it began to pour. Ethan was afraid he had his answer. He couldn't.

Clara was up early the next morning. She knew her eyes were still puffy from crying, but she thought her tears were over. They were, until she saw Ethan drive through the yard on his way out to the walnut grove. He didn't stop at the house. He didn't even look her way. She was standing at her bedroom window. If he had looked up, what would she have seen in his face?

She turned away from the window. She wouldn't

see love and that was what she wanted to see more than she wanted her next breath. She was grateful that her sisters had rallied around her. Other than Lizzie, they kept their opinions about Ethan to themselves. Lizzie had no problem pointing out that Clara could do much better.

The dark sky and distant rumbles of thunder made the day pass in slow motion as Clara went over and over Ethan's words yesterday.

In the afternoon, as she lay across her bed pretending to study the eighth-grade mathematics book, Lily came into the room looking for her. "Clara, will you read me a story?"

"Not now, sweetie, I have to study."

"Okay." The word was drawn out and pitiful sounding. Lily slowly shuffled toward the door.

"Come here." Clara patted the bed.

Lily dashed to her side and jumped on the bed. "What story shall we read?"

"I don't have time to read a story. I just wanted a hug."

Lily threw her arms around Clara's neck and squeezed. "Like this?"

"That is perfect. Thank you. Go keep an eye on your brothers for me."

"Okay." Lily tumbled off the bed and went running out the door.

Clara sat up and sighed deeply. Had she made a mistake? Should she have accepted Ethan's proposal? He might grow to love her in time. Until then, she would have the unconditional love of the children to ease her bruised heart.

Would it be enough?

What happened when the children were grown and Ethan still didn't love her? Could she face a lifetime of that? No, she couldn't.

She had made the right decision even if it didn't feel that way.

Lizzie poked her head in the door. "*Daadi* and Naomi are going into town to visit Emma and Adam. Naomi wants to know if you'd like to ride along. Get out for a little while."

"No, I'm fine. You can go if you want."

"Betsy and Greta are going, but I think I'll stay home."

"I don't need a babysitter."

"You're not getting a babysitter. I'm having too much fun playing with the boys in the barn. I've rigged up a rope so we can swing out and drop into a pile of hay. Come join us."

"Maybe later."

Lizzie walked over and gave Clara a hug. "I understand. It will work out as God wants it to."

"I know. Ethan and I were friends. I don't want that to slip away from us. I'll speak to him tonight. If I can without crying."

"You're stronger than you know."

Lizzie left the room and Clara stared at her reflection in the window. "I doubt that."

"Something is wrong."

Hours later, Clara stood staring into the night on her grandfather's front porch. Flashes of lightning in the distance were followed by rumbles of thunder that grew louder with each passing moment. Ethan should have been back long before now.

Lizzie came to stand beside Clara. "Maybe he decided to stay put tonight."

"Not with a storm coming. He wouldn't keep his precious horses out in such weather. Something's wrong. I just know it."

A shift in the wind brought sprinkles of rain splattering on the wooden porch. Lizzie took a step back. "I know you're worried, but come inside and worry. You're going to get soaked out here."

Clara followed her sister inside but she didn't close the door. Where was Ethan? Why hadn't he come to collect the children? She folded her arms tightly across her middle. Something was wrong. "I'm going to go look for him."

"Don't be foolish. He could come driving in any moment."

A rush of wind whipped back Clara's *kapp.* She reached up to hold it in place. "Put the children to bed, Lizzie. I'm going to look for him."

"You don't even know where to start," Lizzie said.

"I know where he's working." Neither one of them had heard Micah come to the kitchen.

Clara walked to him and laid a hand on his shoulder. "Can you tell me how to get up there?"

"*Nee,* but I can show you. It's in a ravine above the lake. We should get going."

"Clara, you can't take the boy out there. What am I saying? *You* can't go out in there. Listen to the wind. It'll be pouring soon. Ethan is fine. He's in God's hands."

Lizzie was right, but Clara couldn't shake the feeling that Ethan needed her. That God needed her to go to him.

Micah took her hand. "He wouldn't keep the horses out in bad weather."

"That's exactly what I said. Get a coat and see if there's a pair of boots that will fit you on the back porch. The ones closest to the door are mine. Bring them here. And bring *Daadi's* raincoat for me, too. It's hanging behind the door."

He nodded and took off.

Clara went back to the front porch. The rain was coming down in buckets now. The heavy drone of it on the roof gave her pause. Lizzie came to the door. "At least wait until the storm is past."

Clara shook her head. "The paper said to expect heavy rain all night. I don't think it's going to let up. Please stay with the little ones. Lily doesn't like storms."

A bolt of lightning lit up the sky and was followed by a deafening clap of thunder. Micah appeared at her side. "That's because *Mamm* and *Daed* were struck by lightning."

Clara took the coat from him and knelt with her hands on his shoulders. "You don't have to come. You can stay here and take care of them."

"If you are going, I'm coming with you. That's what *Onkel* Ethan would want me to do."

Pulling on her boots, Clara slipped into the dark green rubber coat and pulled the hood over her head. Lizzie brought her a pair of flashlights. "What should I do if Ethan comes while you're out in this?"

Clara rose to her feet. "I hope he does. Tell him to stay here. We'll check where he was cutting. If he's not there, we'll come back."

"Something tells me he won't listen to reason, either. You two will be traipsing through the hills passing each other in the dark until daybreak."

"And you can tell me 'I told you so' tomorrow morning."

Dressed in boots and waterproof coats, Clara and Micah left the house. Guided by flashes of lightning and the flashlights, they made their way toward the lake. By the time they reached the shore, the wind had died down and the rumble of thunder had moved on, but the rain continued unabated. The ground, saturated by rains earlier in the week, didn't hold the water. Every gully and ditch was running full, forcing Clara and Micah to find safe crossings as they made their way up into the foothills.

At one point, Micah stopped. He moved his torch one way and then swept it in the other direction.

"What's wrong?" Clara asked.

"I'm not sure which way to go. It looks so different at night."

She had put a huge burden on a very young boy. "Take your time, Micah. You said Ethan was working above the lake."

"There was a ravine that led back into the hills. It made a little waterfall where it went into the lake."

Clara shielded her eyes against the rain to study their surroundings. Over the sound of the rain came the sound of gushing water. "I think I hear the waterfall." It didn't sound like a little waterfall. It sounded like a rushing torrent.

She made her way toward the sound and her fears were realized. The stream was overflowing its banks. She wasn't sure they could make their way alongside it.

"It's this way," Micah said. "See the *X* on the tree? That means that *Onkel* Ethan plans to cut this one down."

Clara could just make out a path between the trees. "All right. I'll go first. You stay close behind me, and we will both stay away from the water."

The path was steep and slippery. Clara struggled to hold her light and keep her balance. She looked up ahead just as lightning flashed across the sky, illuminating a huge horse towering over her. The animal snorted and rolled its eyes in fear. Clara stumbled backward and pressed a hand to her mouth.

Micah worked his way around her. "It's okay. It's just Dutch. Fred is here, too."

With her heart hammering in her chest, Clara approached the animals. "But where's Ethan?"

She didn't see his light or any sign of him. She began shouting his name. The third time she yelled, she heard a faint reply. "Micah, stay with the horses."

Clara moved higher into the woods and called again. This time, she was sure she heard him, but the sound was coming from downhill. Making her way toward the creek, she still didn't see him. "Ethan, where are you?"

"I'm here."

The sound came from below her. She swung her light in that direction and saw his boot protruding from beneath a fallen tree. *Dear God, please don't let him be hurt.*

She made her way around the log and found herself standing in water. Ethan was lying on his back at the edge of the creek. His leg was pinned under the log. The rising water was swirling a few inches away from him. She sloshed to his side. "Ethan, how badly are you hurt?"

"I'm pinned, and my ankle is badly twisted, but I don't think it's broken. You shouldn't be here, Clara. It's too dangerous to be out in the storm."

"A lecture on safety from a man pinned under a tree. You can scold me after I get you out of here." She put her shoulder against the log and tried to move it. It didn't budge. She looked around for something to leverage the weight off him but there was nothing. She made a circuit around the log searching for a way to move it. Finding nothing, she went back to Ethan. She was horrified to see the rising water was just touching his hair.

"I have to get you out. What do I do, Ethan?"

He raised up on his elbows. "Stay calm. You can't move this log by yourself. The chain snapped and my team ran off. I couldn't get out of the way fast enough. You'll have to go get help."

She looked at the water. "You don't have that much time, Ethan. Look how fast it's rising!"

"Believe me, I've been noticing. Don't worry about me, just go get help."

She fell to her knees beside him in the mud. "I can't leave you like this."

He took hold of her hand. "Yes, you can. You have two options, Clara. You can go get help or watch me drown."

He was so calm. How could he be so calm?

"Don't say that." Her breath came in ragged gulps. This couldn't be happening. *Please, God, save him. I love him so much.*

"You're going to run home and get your grandfather. He'll know what to do."

She shook her head. There wasn't time.

He fell back in resignation. His head splashed water on her skirt. She looked up and shouted, "Make it stop raining, God. Make it stop." She jumped up and began trying to push the log aside. "Maybe it will float off you when it gets deep enough."

"It will."

She heard the resignation in his voice. He would already be dead by the time that happened. She kept pushing, but the log wouldn't budge. She beat on it with her hands. Then she fell to her knees and began scooping mud away from the side of his body. "Maybe I can dig you out."

He grabbed her hands. "Clara, listen to me. I praise God for giving me the chance to say this. I love you, Clara. I've never loved anyone the way I love you. I'm sorry it has to be like this."

"No, no, no. Your team is down the hill. Micah is with them. Tell me what to do."

He wiped the rain out of his face and raised up again. She saw a glimmer of hope in his eyes. "Go get them and bring them here. No, wait. Don't let Micah see me like this. Send him for help."

Clara nodded and raced down the hill. Micah was still standing patiently by the horses. She started to reach for Dutch's bridle. He snorted and tossed his head. She stumbled backward. "I can't do this."

Micah came to her side. "What's wrong, Clara. Did you find *Onkel* Ethan? Is he okay?"

He was, but not for long. "Our Father who art in heaven, give me the courage I need." She closed her eyes and reached up. She felt the horse's soft nose. "Just like Buttercup's nose. You're just like Buttercup. I'm not scared of you."

She was, but she opened her eyes, grasped the reins and looked at Micah. The last thing she wanted him to see was Ethan's death. "Can one horse pull a log ten feet?" That was all she needed—ten feet.

"If it isn't too big."

It wasn't. It couldn't be. "Which horse is stronger?"

"Dutch."

She looked at Micah. "A log has fallen on Ethan. I can't move it, but Dutch can. I want you to take Fred and ride as fast as you can to the Weaver's sawmill. She pointed toward a distant hill. "It's just over that rise. There's a gate in the fence at the top. Bring the Weaver men here as fast as you can."

He nodded and she lifted him onto the back of the horse. Quickly, she unhooked the team from each other and the logging arch and smacked Fred's rump. He took off with Micah clinging to his like a flea.

She grabbed Dutch's reins with trembling hands and led the horse toward Ethan. When she reached him she saw only swirling water where he had been. "Ethan!" she screamed.

A second later, he pushed up out of the water and coughed. "My arms got tired. I had to rest."

"Don't do that again. I've sent Micah on Fred to go get help."

"That's *goot.*"

"How do I hook Dutch up?"

He gave her careful instructions, but without the arch and with a broken chain, she had to improvise. She had no idea if it would hold but there was no time to try anything else. She went to Dutch's head. From the corner of her eye, she could see Ethan straining to keep his head above water. She laid her forehead against the horse's face. "It's all up to you now. Save him."

Grasping the reins, she got uphill of the log and gave Dutch the command to pull. He lurched into his collar. The log barely moved. She looked for Ethan, but she couldn't see him.

"Hup, Dutch! Hup!" she yelled.

The big horse lunged into this collar, straining so hard he was almost on his knees, but the log gave and began to swing in her direction. Was it enough? She raced around the end. She couldn't see Ethan.

waded into the water, calling his name, feeling for him in the muck.

"Here," came a weak call.

She spun around. He was several feet downstream, hauling himself out of the water. She ran to him and put her shoulder under his arm to give him leverage. "Thank You, God. Thank you, Dutch."

Ethan was wet and shivering. She took her coat off. It was wet, but it still held some of her warmth for they were both soaking wet. Her *kapp* was long gone and her bun had come undone, spilling her hair down her back. She wrapped her coat around Ethan and sat beside him on the muddy ground. He wiped his face with the back of the sleeve. "That was exciting."

She punched his arm.

"Ouch. That's my sore arm."

"Sorry. Don't joke about this. Ever."

He opened the coat so she could scoot in closer to him and they could share their body warmth. "I won't joke about it, but it was almost worth it to get you in my arms."

Clara glared at him. He managed not to smile. She was so beautiful with her hair down and smears of mud on her cheeks. "I'm going to kiss you now. Punch the other arm if it makes you mad."

She looked away from him. "I said no jokes."

"Honey, this is no joke. I spoke the truth earlie

"Did you mean it when you said that you love me?" She sounded so insecure. He had to make her see that she was everything he'd ever wanted.

He sighed deeply. "I was mistaken when I asked you to marry me."

He saw her flinch and hurried on. "You were right to refuse me. I thought our mutual love for the children, our friendship and our shared faith was enough for us to start a life together."

She fixed her gaze on the water rushing below them. If only she would look at him. "I'm sorry that I hurt you, Clara. I never meant to do that."

"And I'm sorry if my refusal hurt your feelings. I hope we can still be friends. For the sake of the children."

"Please look at me, Clara. I know you have the courage to hear what I have to say."

When she met his gaze, he continued, "You forced me to take a closer look at my feelings. I didn't want to marry you because of the children or for any other reason. Clara, I wanted to marry you because you are a pearl beyond price. I didn't see that because I was afraid."

"Of what?"

"I was afraid of being hurt, of finding out once again that the person I loved didn't love me back. My mother didn't love me enough to take me with

r. Jenny didn't love me enough. I thought I was roken somehow, that no one could love me."

She cupped his face with her hands. "You aren't broken."

"I was, and you fixed me."

"Oh, Ethan, I didn't do anything."

"You did. You showed me what true love was like. Even if you don't love me, I will always treasure the things you have taught me."

"I love you, too, Ethan. I can't imagine loving someone more."

Relief swept away what little strength he had left. He wrapped his arms around her and held her close. "Thank you, darling. Thank you."

Clara raised her face for his kiss. His lips closed tenderly over hers and her heart sang with such joy that it stole her breath away. When he drew back, he tucked her head against his throat and cradled her. She sighed with happiness. "Ask the question."

"What question?" She heard the hint of humor in his tone.

"Don't make me punch your arm again. Ask the question."

"Clara Barkman, will you do me the honor of becoming my wife? For better, for worse, for richer, for poorer, in sickness and with a passel of naughty *kinder* to boot?"

She pulled away to face him. She wanted to see

the look in his eyes when she gave her answer. will marry you on one condition."

"I won't get smaller horses, and that's final."

"Dutch is okay. My condition is that we never, ever, tell the children how close they came to losing you tonight."

"I agree. Now, will you marry me?"

She leaned in for his kiss. "Yes. I did not do all this work tonight for nothing."

When his tender kiss ended, Clara snuggled against him with a sigh of contentment. God had opened her eyes to what love should be between a man and a woman and she gave thanks for His blessing. Nothing had ever felt so right.

She remained in Ethan's arms, content to stay there forever, but eventually she saw lights approaching through the trees and heard the shouts of Mr. Weaver and his sons. She pressed a hand to her heart and gave thanks again. Micah had reached them safely.

Ethan shouted to let the searchers know where they were.

"What a good, brave boy Micah is," she said.

"Brave like his new mother," Ethan said quietly.

"I'm not brave. God gave me the strength when I needed it."

"I guess this means the school board will have to find another teacher."

"Yes," she replied without hesitation. "I think Melinda Miller will be perfect for the job."

"I know you would have made a wonderful teacher, but I can't imagine my life without you. God has given me the greatest gift."

She would love and cherish Ethan and his children forever, and she would never stop thanking God for bringing them into her life. This was the path He had chosen for her.

This was where she was meant to be.

* * * * *

Dear Reader,

Once again, I've had the chance to return to the Amish community in Hope Springs, Ohio. Every time I travel there, I learn something new about the Amish and about myself.

I have always had a great love of horses. I think that may have been one thing that drew me to the Amish genre in the first place. I'm not a big fan of no electricity, however. In researching this book, I learned so much about the draft horses that are used by many Amish in farmwork. They are truly awesome animals. Here in Kansas, the Amish use tractors. It simply isn't feasible to farm the large tracts of land necessary to produce the same amount of crops that can be grown in places like Ohio, where the rainfall is higher.

If you are wondering where I came up with the idea of Ethan being trapped and threatened by rising water, I must tell you the idea occurred to me before the devastating flooding that struck my state and the neighboring state of Colorado in 2013. Disasters will always happen. Wonderful people will always respond with incredible bravery. We never know what we can do until we are tested and that is what I wanted Clara to learn.

I hope you enjoyed the story, and be sure to look for my next Brides of Amish Country novel

Christmas. At the time I wrote this letter, I didn't have a title, but you can check for more information on my website at www.patriciadavids.com.

Blessings,

Patricia Davids

Questions for Discussion

1. Ethan had been abandoned by his mother when he was young and he carried that fear with him throughout his life. How can we overcome such deep-rooted fears in ourselves?

2. Because of Ethan's upbringing, he was ill prepared to raise his brother's children. What are some of the mistakes he made? How could he have changed this?

3. What character did you identify with most closely in the story?

4. Ethan quickly came to rely on Clara's instincts with the children. Is there someone who was a mentor to you when you were bringing up your own children?

5. How did that person change you as a parent?

6. Clara is surrounded by loving sisters. It would be nice if all siblings were like this, but they aren't. How would you change your relationship with your siblings if you could?

role of the teacher in Amish society is different from what we expect in our public education. Do you agree or disagree with the decision that Amish teachers have no formal education beyond the eighth grade?

8. If you are familiar with the Brides of Amish Country series, which book have you found most interesting and why?

9. What themes were emphasized in this novel?

10. If you took away one message from this novel, what was it and why?

11. The use of horses for logging purposes is a practice that is hundreds of years old. A few dedicated men and women still work this way. Do you know anyone who has a team of draft horses?

12. What was the funniest scene in this book? Why do you feel that way?

13. What was the most poignant scene in this book? What touched you the most and why?

14. The Amish do not allow married women to be teachers. This was a common practice in

the United States until the turn of the cent
What benefits or detriments do you see fro
only having single women teach children?

15. If you were to choose one character from this book to have a story written about, which character would it be and why?